"Hi. I'm ...
name?"

The little girl popped her free thumb into her mouth. A second later her thumb shot out of her mouth and she fleetingly touched Allie's dress. "Pretty."

"Thank you. Your dress is pretty, too."

The little girl lovingly patted the acres of skirt. "Daddy bought it."

"Who is your daddy?" Allie asked.

The child looked past Allie. Her face lit up like a million candles. "He's my daddy." She pointed up.

"Hello, Allie."

Allie's heart stopped. The room went dim. Her body froze and she forgot to breathe.

What was Zane Peters doing here?

Dear Reader,

Sitting in my red-wallpapered office, I'm surrounded by family photographs. I love seeing my husband as a baby, my father as an adolescent and my daughter at age four holding her new baby brother.

For better or worse, we all have families. I didn't plan to write about the Lassiter family, but as one character formed in my mind I realized I was dealing with all three Lassiter sisters—Cheyenne, Allie and Greeley. Then their older brother demanded his story be told, and who can say no to a sexy man like Worth Lassiter? What started out as one book had suddenly become four.

I hope you enjoy reading about the Lassiter family and the strong men—and woman!—who match them.

Love

Jeanne Allan

Four weddings, one Colorado family

One Mother Wanted
Jeanne Allan

HOPE VALLEY BRIDES

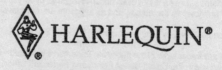

HARLEQUIN®

TORONTO • NEW YORK • LONDON
AMSTERDAM • PARIS • SYDNEY • HAMBURG
STOCKHOLM • ATHENS • TOKYO • MILAN • MADRID
PRAGUE • WARSAW • BUDAPEST • AUCKLAND

ISBN 0-373-15822-X

ONE MOTHER WANTED

First North American Publication 1999.

Visit us at www.romance.net

Printed in U.S.A.

CHAPTER ONE

THE Augusta Room in the century-old, Steele-owned St. Christopher Hotel in Aspen, Colorado provided the perfect backdrop for the wedding reception of Thomas Steele and Cheyenne Lassiter. Autumn had cooled the September afternoon enough to permit fires in the carved Art Nouveau fireplaces at either end of the huge ballroom. Slender metal pillars encircled the room, while chandeliers hanging from the two-story-high vaulted ceiling bathed the room's occupants with a soft pink glow as friends, neighbors and relatives toasted the happy couple. Curious hotel guests and tourists who'd wandered in from the street to see the historic ballroom found themselves accepting flutes of champagne and gawking at the movie stars, business tycoons, sports figures and politicians moving easily through the throng. Immense arrangements of creamy pink roses, white lilies and herbs, such as marjoram for joy and happiness, myrtle for love and passion, ivy for friendship and sage for long life, perfumed the air.

Alberta Harmony Lassiter could hardly wait to leave.

"Allie, aren't you ready to go yet?" The boyish voice rang with desperation. "Cheyenne, I mean, Mom, said we didn't have to stay forever."

Allie smiled at her new nephew. Davy Steele had been an infant when his parents died in a plane crash. Cheyenne told him his mother would always be his mother, but if he wanted to call Cheyenne "Mom," he could. Davy had eagerly embraced the idea.

Tousling the seven-year-old's hair, Allie said, "We have to wait until they cut the cake and all that stuff."

"Do we have to? That'll take forever."

"Yes, we have to. Since you'll be staying on the ranch with Mom and Worth and Greeley, you'll have plenty of time to ride horses while Cheyenne and Thomas are on their honeymoon."

Honeymoon. It didn't seem possible. It was a matter of weeks since Allie's sister had met Davy and his Uncle Thomas. Today Cheyenne had become Mrs. Thomas Steele and Davy's mother. Davy would undoubtedly soon call Thomas "Dad."

Allie's eyes grew damp. Her older sister married with a ready-made family. Cheyenne made a beautiful bride. Her sister's beauty transcended mere physical appearance. Cheyenne's glowing beauty came from within. The kind of beauty that came from being deeply loved.

Once Allie had thought she was loved like that. She'd been wrong.

"Oh, no, here she comes."

The muttered words of dismay reminded Allie of the boy at her side. "Who comes?"

"Her." He pointed toward a small girl trotting in their direction, a shy smile on her face. "I can't get away from her."

Despite a sense of familiarity, Allie had never seen the child before. Curly red ringlets framed a cherubic face. "She doesn't look dangerous to me." She looked about four years old.

Davy gave Allie a disgusted look. "She keeps bothering me." The little girl reached for his hand and he jerked it from her grasp. "Go away. I don't like girls."

Giant tears welled up in the child's eyes.

"See?" Davy appealed to Allie. "She does that every time I tell her to go away. Stop crying," he said to the girl. "We're going to have cake. Don't you like cake?"

The girl nodded and reached out her hand again. With a huge sigh, Davy took it.

Giving Davy a smile in which commiseration mingled with approval, Allie crouched down so her face was level with the child's. "Hi. I'm Allie and this is Davy. What's your name?"

The little girl popped her free thumb into her mouth.

"She won't talk," Davy said. "Maybe she don't know how."

The child gave him an indignant look.

Allie swallowed a laugh. "Do you like weddings?"

The child shrugged. A second later her thumb shot out of her mouth and she fleetingly touched Allie's dress. "Pretty."

"Thank you. Your dress is pretty, too." The neon pink monstrosity of ruffles and ribbons was too big and the wrong color. A torn ruffle had been inexpertly mended.

The little girl lovingly patted the acres of skirt. "Daddy bought it."

"Who is your daddy?" Allie asked.

The child looked past Allie. Her face lit up like a million candles. "He's my daddy." She pointed up.

"Hello, Allie."

Allie's heart stopped. The room went dim. Her body froze and she forgot to breathe. What was Zane Peters doing here? He couldn't be here. Not at a wedding. Not when she once believed she'd be the first Lassiter sister to marry. Believed she'd marry him. How dare he show up uninvited at Cheyenne's wedding? How dare he speak to Allie? He couldn't possibly think she'd forgiven him.

She'd never forgive him. He'd hurt her more than any person had a right to hurt another. Past tense. He no longer had the power to hurt her. He had no power over her at all.

"Allie? You okay? You look kinda funny. Can't you get up? Want me to get Grandma Mary or Cheyenne, I mean, Mom?"

Davy's anxious voice snapped Allie from her trance. "No." Her voice came out sharply. Giving

Davy a smile she hoped was reassuring, Allie said, "I'm okay. My foot went to sleep."

"Let me help you up," Zane said.

She ignored his offer and his extended hand. Standing, Allie saw her older sister across the room. Concern covered Cheyenne's face. And guilt.

Darn Cheyenne. For five years Allie had managed to avoid Zane Peters. She'd taught school in Denver, and when in Aspen, she'd developed a kind of radar that prevented chance encounters.

Without once looking at the man who had betrayed her, Allie headed straight for her sister.

"I can explain," Cheyenne said, as soon as Allie reached her. "Zane was Worth's best friend."

"I'm Worth's sister." Allie paused. "Are you telling me Worth invited him?"

Cheyenne's color heightened. "I saw Zane in town yesterday. He said 'hello' so cautiously, it would have been funny if it wasn't so sad. You've told me a million times you don't care about him anymore. That he's nothing to you. But he was one of our oldest friends, and Worth misses him."

"He's never said so to me."

"Worth wouldn't. Okay, so he's never said anything to me, either, but they were best friends forever."

Allie hadn't been born yesterday. "And that's the only reason you invited him? For Worth?" She watched her sister's face. Cheyenne had never been able to tell a convincing lie.

"Why else? I know you're not interested in him."

Proper decorum prevented one from strangling a bride on her wedding day, even if she was the lyingest bride that ever said her vows. "You know I hate it when you stick your pointed nose into my business."

Red flagged Cheyenne's cheeks. "It's no more pointed than yours. Besides—" she looked somewhere in the vicinity of Allie's forehead "—his wife is dead. You and Zane could—"

"Could nothing. You listen to me, Cheyenne Lassiter, if you want to be some stupid man's doormat, go ahead. I don't, so mind your own cotton-picking business."

"Personally I can't see my wife being anyone's doormat." A solid arm snaked around Allie's waist.

"If you hadn't been warned," she said to a smiling Thomas Steele, "I'd feel sorry for you. The rest of us are stuck with her, but you could have walked away."

"I may be a stupid man, but I can guess what's going on."

"I'm sorry I called you stupid—" mortification heated Allie's face "—but sometimes my sister..."

"What did Ms. Busybody do now?" Thomas smiled at his bride. "I love you, Mrs. Steele, but that doesn't mean I'm blind to your interfering ways."

Cheyenne looked so penitent, Allie shook her head. "It doesn't matter." She summoned up a big smile. "I was surprised and overreacted. It isn't every day my big sister gets married. I guess I'm a little emotional."

Cheyenne gave her a big hug. "Liar," she whispered in Allie's ear. Taking Allie's hands in hers, out loud she said, "I blew it. It won't happen again. I promise. Cross my heart."

Allie gave an unladylike snort and they both laughed.

Thomas looked from one to the other. "I'm never going to understand women, am I?"

"That's what puts the fun in marriage," Allie's mother teased as she joined them. "My new grandson is going to go berserk if you two don't hurry up and cut the wedding cake so he and Allie can head for the ranch. Davy rates riding horses much higher than weddings," Mary Lassiter added with a laugh.

Short hair suited her.

She smiled at the groom. Once she'd reserved her warmest smiles for Zane. He'd fallen in love with Allie Lassiter ten years ago. Many things had changed, but not that. Never that.

He had no right to love her, not after what he'd done. He didn't expect her to welcome him back into her life. Or her arms. Which didn't stop him from indulging in fantasies.

"Starving dogs don't look that hungrily at food."

Zane didn't need to turn to identify the speaker. "When I ran into Cheyenne yesterday and she invited me to her wedding, I thought maybe..." He uttered a short, bitter laugh. "Allie didn't know I was coming. Cheyenne didn't tell her."

"Cheyenne couldn't have gotten married without both her sisters in attendance," Worth Lassiter said.

"Meaning Allie would have stayed away rather than meet me. How about you? Would Cheyenne have walked down the aisle alone if you'd known I was coming?"

"I knew. Cheyenne had second thoughts and asked me if she should phone you and take back the invitation. Then she decided you wouldn't come. I knew you would."

Zane couldn't decipher Worth's tone of voice. Nor could he bring himself to look at this man who'd been his best friend. "We had some good times together, you and I."

"Yeah." Worth added quietly, "I've missed you, you son of a gun, but Allie's my sister. What you did about killed her."

Zane said fiercely, "I'd do anything, pay any price, if I could undo what I did."

"I know."

Zane looked at Worth. "Does she?"

Worth shrugged. "She hasn't spoken your name to me since the night she walked into the house and told us you were marrying someone else."

"I thought she'd be married by now."

"Men have been interested. She's not. Between Beau and you, Allie's opinion of men isn't too high."

Zane shoved clenched fists in his pockets. Men didn't come much lower than Beau Lassiter, Allie's late and unlamented father. Yet Zane couldn't deny the truth of Worth's words, no matter how painful they were. "Hannah's been looking forward to the cake, but we'd better leave."

"I never knew you had a yellow streak a mile wide down your back." Worth walked away.

Zane watched his former friend cross the room. Worth had called him a coward. Zane had no idea why.

Laughter caught his attention. Allie and her two sisters laughed with the groom. Zane used to dream about her laughing in his bed. Although he'd tossed away the right to have those kind of dreams, the dreams had never stopped.

Hannah had wandered off again, but he kept her in sight. She stood near the bridal party, her big blue eyes locked on Allie. Little girls were supposed to be crazy about weddings, but Hannah appeared fascinated by the maid of honor instead of the bride.

Most people thought the two older Lassiter sisters looked alike. They couldn't be more wrong. Cheyenne was an open book. Allie was a closed book, with only a precious few allowed to peek inside. Once Zane had been privileged to share her innermost thoughts. A privilege he'd stupidly thrown away. Even from across St. Chris's ballroom, he could see how shuttered her face was, how hidden her thoughts and emotions. If he were a man given to crying, he'd cry now. He could have cried a million times over the past five years. Crying wouldn't have changed a thing.

Neither would running. He'd stay until Hannah had her cake. Then he'd get the hell out of here. Away from Allie Lassiter.

Jake Norton joined the bridal party and put his arms around Allie and her sister Greeley. Zane had read in the newspaper about Norton and his wife staying on the Lassiter ranch while the movie star filmed a Western in the area. He knew the couple had become close friends with the Lassiters. The knowledge did nothing to stop the jealousy that rocketed through Zane as Allie laughed up at Norton.

He'd been an idiot to come. If only the bride would cut the damned cake. Not that he'd be able to choke any down. Just cut it, so Hannah could have her piece. Then he could leave.

She was so damned beautiful. More beautiful than five years ago. He could almost taste her mouth. His own went dry. Cut the damned cake.

Allie wanted to scream. They'd cut the cake, and everyone had toasted the newlyweds. Brides were supposed to be anxious to leave on their honeymoons. Thomas ought to be chomping at the bit to get Cheyenne to himself. If Cheyenne would throw the darned bouquet, Allie could escape. She had to get out of here.

Out of this clinging blue floral silk dress that had seemed so elegantly simple and classic when she'd put it on earlier. Now the dress felt wrong. Too tight. If he didn't quit watching her... She couldn't stand being in the same room with him.

"I assume you know Zane's here. I just saw him. You okay?" Greeley asked quietly at her side.

Allie turned to her younger sister. "Of course I'm okay," she said brightly. "Why wouldn't I be?"

"How would I know? I'm just your half sister."

"Greeley Lassiter, you are as much my sister as Cheyenne is. You make me furious when you say such stupid things."

"That's better than you standing there looking like the sole, dazed survivor of some disaster."

"I don't look like that," Allie said in a low, fierce voice. At Greeley's skeptical look, she added, "It was a shock, that's all. I didn't know Cheyenne had invited him."

"I thought I detected the hand of our resident meddler. Want me to tell him to take a hike?"

"Worth talked to him."

"And told him to leave?"

"Obviously not. They seemed to be just talking. They didn't shake hands or anything."

"I should hope not."

Allie gave her sister a quick squeeze of appreciation for her loyalty. "No, Cheyenne is right. If he no longer matters to me, he and Worth should be able to resume their friendship. If Worth wants such a shallow friend."

"*If,*" Greeley emphasized the word, "he no longer matters?"

"He doesn't matter," Allie said firmly. He couldn't matter. Their love had died. Not died, been trampled in the dirt. Nothing remained. Nothing. She forced a smile to her face. "Cheyenne's finally ready to throw the bouquet. You know she'll aim it over here. You catch it, because I'm not going to."

Sent on its way with teasing comments, the bridal bouquet arced through the air. Directly toward Allie and Greeley. Allie stepped to her right at the exact second Greeley stepped to her left. The bouquet sailed between them.

"Look, Daddy! The lady threw flowers to me."

One look at Cheyenne's dismayed face confirmed Allie's suspicions about her older sister's intent.

"I'm not getting involved in this." Greeley strolled away before Allie could ask what she meant.

"Are mine," came a determined voice from behind Allie.

She turned.

Zane crouched inches away, speaking to his daughter. The little girl clutched the bridal bouquet to her chest and shook her head. "Mine."

He held out his hand. "No, they're not. The flowers are for a big girl."

"I'm a big girl."

"They're for a lady," Zane amended. "Give these back to the bride, and we'll go to a flower shop and buy you some flowers."

"I caught 'em."

"You weren't supposed to."

The little girl's mouth wobbled. "I want 'em."

Allie wanted to smile indulgently like everyone else watching the scene. The high color on Zane's face told her he knew he and his daughter were the focus of attention. Not that that would stop him from doing what he thought was right. Zane Peters prided himself on doing what he thought was right.

He wrested the flowers from his daughter's grasp and awkwardly wiped a tear from her cheek. "We can buy yellow flowers. You like yellow flowers." Desperation edged his voice.

Red curls bounced as the little girl shook her head. "Don't want yellow flowers. Want these."

Without stopping to think, Allie leaned over and jerked the bouquet from Zane. Turning her back to him, she offered the flowers to the little girl. "Here. You caught them."

The little girl put her hands behind her back. "Daddy said I can't have 'em."

Allie wanted nothing to do with Zane's daughter, but the girl had caught the bouquet and should be allowed to keep it. Allie knelt on the floor. "Your daddy is a man, and men know nothing about weddings. Whoever catches the bouquet keeps it. It's a rule, and I know your daddy doesn't believe in breaking rules." Allie coated the last sentence with deliberate mockery.

The little girl looked at the floor and shook her head. Her hands stayed behind her. "Daddy said flowers for a big lady."

"I'm a big lady. May I have the flowers?"

The little girl hesitated, then nodded sadly.

"All right, if they are my flowers, I may give them to someone else, and I'm giving them to you." Allie held out the bouquet, proving she could act with dignity and fairness, no matter the circumstances.

The little girl started to bring her hands forward, stopped and looked past Allie in her father's direction. Then, smiling shyly, she accepted the bouquet and buried her face in a large lily. "Pretty." She held the bouquet to Allie's face. "Smell."

Hoping compliance would make the child and her father go away, Allie sniffed.

"What do you say, Hannah?" Zane prompted.

"Thank you."

Hannah. Unbelievable pain slashed through Allie. The child had been named after his grandmother. They'd planned to name their first daughter Hannah. This little girl could be, should be, Allie's daughter. Allie's throat ached with the effort not to cry, then hot, burning anger replaced the pain. He'd taken "their name" and used it for that woman's daughter. Not that it mattered anymore. He didn't matter anymore.

"Allie, aren't you ready yet?"

Davy's impatient voice rescued her. She smiled gratefully at him. "Ready and raring to go."

The child's hand tugging on her arm kept Allie from rising. "You his mommy?"

Allie shook her head as Davy pointed to

Cheyenne and said proudly, "She's my mom now. That makes Allie my aunt."

"Whose mommy?" Zane's daughter asked.

"I don't have any children," Allie said stiffly.

"How come? They playing with angels?"

"Let's go, Hannah," Zane said in a rough voice.

"But Daddy, maybe her kids know Mommy."

Zane snatched up his daughter and walked away.

A hand gripped Allie's shoulder. "You okay?" Worth asked.

"Why does everyone keep asking me that?"

"Davy said you looked funny."

"Davy thinks I look funny every time he sees me in a dress," Allie said to her brother, trying to make a joke of it. "He says I look like a girl." She mimicked the disgusted tone of Davy's voice. "He wants me in jeans because I promised him we'd ride horses after the wedding. Where'd Davy go? He was in such a hurry to leave."

"Last minute hugs and kisses from the bride and groom."

Loud voices caught Allie's attention. "They must be leav..." Her voice died as she spotted the cause of the commotion.

Zane's daughter was throwing a grade-A tantrum in her father's arms. Hanging on to her bouquet with one hand, she used her other hand to cling to one of the stylized metal Art Nouveau pillars. Zane's face turned the shade of cooked beets as onlookers tittered with laughter. The child drummed his side with her feet. "I want down," she howled.

Setting his daughter on the floor, Zane grabbed in vain for her hand as she darted across the ballroom. The little girl skidded to a stop in front of Allie, still kneeling on the floor. Throwing her arms around Allie's neck, Zane's daughter pressed an enthusiastic kiss on Allie's cheek. "Bye." The little girl spun around and dashed back to her father, her childish voice floating across the ballroom. "I had to tell Allie bye."

The rest of his life without Allie. How long must he pay? Hadn't he been punished enough? Zane had had five long years to think about the answers to those questions. No punishment, no matter how severe or how long, could wipe out what he'd done. Allie's face when he'd told her would forever haunt him.

He'd thought he'd reconciled himself to the devastation he'd wrought. Accepted that Allie would never be part of his life. The minute he saw her at Cheyenne's wedding, he knew he'd been deluding himself.

The crazy idea came to him on the way home from the wedding. There must have been too much sugar in the wedding cake. Or else the smell of those damned flowers had rotted his brain.

For about the hundredth time, Zane picked up the telephone. And put it back down. If he drank, he'd pour himself a huge glass of courage. Except he no longer drank alcohol, and no one knew better than he that drinking made a man stupid, not brave.

At the wedding reception, Allie had avoided looking at him. Not that he was any great shakes to look at. An ordinary guy with black hair and a square jaw. Allie had never seemed to mind the ridiculous dent in his chin.

Smart about everything else, Allie had been stupid when it came to him. Stupid enough to love him. She wouldn't be stupid enough to fall for his pitiful scheme. She wouldn't believe it for a second. She wouldn't do it.

He'd searched long and diligently for the right horse.

Zane rubbed one thumb over the other and eyed the phone. Think about the filly. Damn it, even if he'd royally screwed up his life, the filly deserved help. He'd call.

Allie would hang up on him.

Angrily he pushed the phone aside and rose. Allie roamed through his mind the way she used to roam around his family's ranch. At the uncurtained window, he stared into the black night. Nights were the worst. Thinking about Allie. Remembering. Little things. Like the way she stuck her tongue out of the corner of her mouth when she concentrated. He used to tease her that one day she'd be on a horse, concentrating, and the horse would buck and she'd bite off the end of her tongue.

His body tensed with need. He wanted to nibble that tongue. Gently. Lovingly.

He'd thrown away that privilege. Thrown away love.

Horses moving in the home pasture caught his eye. The filly would be in the middle. She never let herself get isolated. The other horses were her protection. She didn't trust men.

Allie could teach the filly to trust.

If he didn't call, Allie couldn't help the filly. He started to turn toward the phone, then stopped.

If he didn't call, Allie couldn't say no. There was no reason for her to say yes and too many reasons for her to say no. If she said no...

Zane couldn't remember when he hadn't known Allie. At first she was merely one of Worth's sisters. Then she'd turned sixteen, and he found himself falling in love with her. On Allie's eighteenth birthday he asked her to marry him.

Allie's mom asked them to wait. Mary Lassiter had married young. Beau Lassiter had been a rodeo cowboy, long on looks and charm, short on character. Beau had left Mary on her parents' ranch when she became pregnant with Worth. After that, Mary stayed on the ranch while Beau rode the rodeo circuit. Whenever a bull stove him up, Beau would head to the ranch where Mary nursed him back to health. Then Beau returned to the bright lights, alone. More often than not, he left Mary pregnant.

With the help of her widowed father, Yancy Nichols, Mary had raised four kids, Greeley not even hers. No one ever heard a word of complaint from Mary. When Mary asked them to wait, Zane assumed she wanted Allie to be sure. Later he wondered if she'd seen something of Beau in him.

He was nothing like Beau Lassiter.

Hearing the lie, Zane felt like smashing his fist through the window.

He wanted to blame Beau for what happened. Beau, whose irresponsible behavior had rushed his children into adulthood. Six years older than Allie, Zane had often told her she needed to lighten up, to live a little, but she'd been inflexible, and intolerant with youthful high spirits in others. In him.

No. He wouldn't make excuses. The sole responsibility for what had happened belonged to one person. Zane Peters.

He shouldn't have gone to Cheyenne's wedding, but the temptation to see Allie, to speak to her, had been overwhelming. Watching her stand tall and slim beside her sister as Cheyenne said her vows, he'd ached to touch her. When he'd seen her smile at Hannah, he'd craved one of her smiles.

One look at her face told him she hadn't forgiven him. If not for Hannah, he would have left.

She'd been kind to Hannah.

His daughter had rattled on about Allie all the way home. Zane had lost count of the things he regretted, but he'd never regretted Hannah. It wasn't Hannah's fault Allie hated him. He knew who to blame.

So did Allie. Allie would never blame Hannah, because she loved kids and animals.

She'd help the filly. Allie hated him, but she'd help the filly. And then, maybe... Taking a deep breath, Zane dialed.

At the sound of her voice, intense longing swept over him. He couldn't speak.

Allie had polished the kitchen and bathroom, cleaned the cat box and walked Moonie so long the greyhound had practically sighed with relief when they'd returned to the condo. She'd washed windows, done her laundry, baked a loaf of bread and caught up on filing for C & A Enterprises, the small, specialized tour agency she and Cheyenne owned and operated. The night stretched endlessly before her.

She should have stayed in Hope Valley at the Double Nickel, the family ranch named for her great-great-grandparents. Or persuaded Davy to stay in Aspen with her instead of at the ranch. With Cheyenne gone, the condo had too many empty corners. Too much quiet. She needed a roommate. Someone who'd fill the silence. Silence led to thinking. And remembering. Allie didn't want to remember.

As if she'd ever forget.

By the time she was ten, Allie knew every nuance of Zane Peters's walk. She'd memorized his low-pitched laugh and his slow and easy way of talking. The way he'd drawled her name and called her honey had sent shivers down her spine. She'd teased him, telling him he was a Southern boy, not a true Westerner.

The accent came from his Texas-born mother. Dolly Peters had ridden the barrel-racing circuit where she'd become fast friends with Mary Lassiter, and like Mary, had married a rodeo cowboy. The difference was Buck Peters quit the rodeo and came home to his family's ranch near Aspen. Buck and Dolly had moved to Texas when Dolly's aged parents needed them, and now they operated the Texas ranch Dolly had inherited while Zane raised and trained horses and ran some cattle on the Colorado ranch.

Her thoughts always circled back to Zane. If Allie hadn't agreed to her mother's request to wait, she and Zane would have been married almost eight years now.

Or divorced.

Loving Zane hadn't blinded her to his flaws. He had a reckless streak and took too many chances. Allie had been away at school, but reports filtered to her about his partying. She'd worried about him drinking too much and driving too fast on the curving mountain roads back to his ranch. Home on a holiday visit, she'd nagged him; he'd accused her of not trusting him and of asking friends to spy on him. The argument had escalated until she'd ripped off her engagement ring and shoved it in his shirt pocket. Told him to go away, that she'd never marry him.

If he'd apologized, begged her to take back the ring... He hadn't. Without a word, he'd left her standing in front of the ranch house. She'd watched him tear out the gate and down the dirt road, driving so fast his truck fishtailed on the curves.

Her throat ached with angry, unshed tears. She
didn't want to think about Zane. The shock of his
betrayal. The wrenching pain. The slow, agonizing
realization that her life had drastically changed.

Resentment flared. He didn't look like a man
who'd suffered. He looked... She searched for an
acceptable word. He looked well.

The phone rang sharply, startling her and provid-
ing welcome respite from unwanted, bitter memories. When she answered, silence greeted her.
"Hello? Hello? I'm hanging up."

"Don't hang up, Allie. I'm calling about a
horse."

Allie's brain went blank, rendering her incapable
of uttering a word.

"I have this filly who needs help. She's a good-
looking two-year-old who's been mistreated. I've
watched her in the pasture, and she's quick and
smart. She might make a good little cow pony for
Hannah in a few years. I don't think there's an
ounce of vice in her, but she's terrified of people.
I'd like you to work with her. I'm willing to pay
whatever you want."

The uncharacteristic fast-paced flow of words
told her how nervous Zane was. Let him be nervous.
She was hanging up.

"She needs you," Zane said quickly, as if reading Allie's mind. "A man goes near her, she gets
the shimmering shakes so bad, her hide's going to
fall off. I can't use her, and even if Hannah would

let me, I can't sell her. It's not the filly's fault she learned to distrust men.''

"No, it takes a man to teach a female that men are the lowest of scum."

A stark silence met her bitter retort before Zane asked, "Will you help the filly?"

"No."

"You didn't used to hold an owner's behavior against an animal," he said evenly.

Allie wanted to scream he'd destroyed the person she used to be. She said nothing, wrapping the phone cord so tightly around her fist, her fingers ached.

"So much for all your animal-rescue rhetoric."

How dare he try to shame her into helping him?

"Don't worry. Your friends won't find out from me you refused to help an animal in need."

Allie yanked the phone cord tighter around her fingers. His subtle blackmail wouldn't work. Zane could call any number of people to help him with a horse. She had a tour business to run.

Amber strolled into the living room and jumped lightly up onto Allie's lap. Curling into a furry ball, the three-legged cat gave Allie an unblinking yellow-eyed stare. Allie had found the cat abandoned and half-dead beside the highway.

Zane exhaled loudly. "I'm sorry I bothered you."

Stroking Amber's neck, Allie knew she couldn't ignore the filly's plight. "I'm taking a family with a blind child up Independence Pass tomorrow to the

Braille trail and to the ghost town of Independence. I won't be able to get to the Double Nickel until after four. That gives you plenty of time to trailer the filly over to Hope Valley and be gone.''

"I'm not trailering her anywhere. She went crazy coming here. Luckily she didn't injure herself, but I'm not putting her through that again. I'll move her to the round pen by the barn.''

Allie didn't want to go anywhere near Zane's ranch. She didn't want to see Zane again. Amber rolled on her back, presenting her stomach for Allie to rub. The cat bore no resemblance to the pitiful near-skeleton Allie had brought home from the veterinarian's office. Then, Amber had lashed out in a fear-crazed fury at every kind overture.

Taking a deep breath, Allie buried her fingers in Amber's fur. "I'll look at her tomorrow, but I'm not making any promises. There's no reason for you to be there. I'll call you with my answer.'' Allie put down the phone. She'd leave a message on his answering machine. After she found someone else to work with the filly.

Even with Amber's contented purring, thirty minutes passed before Allie quit shaking.

CHAPTER TWO

INCREDIBLY stupid didn't begin to describe Allie driving to Zane Peters's ranch. Ahead of her tourists in a rented vehicle rubbernecked at the palatial homes while the September sunlight sparkled off the creek rushing beside the road. Two deer stood motionless in a mowed field watching a flock of magpies erupt into the sky. The black-and-white birds circled to land on a dead stag high up the ridge. Clumps of aspen trees splashed the hillside with gold.

Curves of the road and breaks in the trees provided glimpses of the Elk Mountains. Normally the sight of the rugged peaks raised Allie's spirits and brought her peace. Not today. Not when she couldn't quit wondering why Zane Peters had telephoned her. Not that his reasons mattered. She'd agreed to see the horse for the horse's sake. Not to renew any kind of relationship with Zane.

Allie had dressed to make that point perfectly clear, digging the stained, worn jeans from the dirty clothes hamper. Moonie had slept on her shirt, an ancient one of Worth's.

Driving slowly into the ranch yard, Allie parked

by the barn. She had no intention of going anywhere near the house.

The horse in the round pen dashed to the far side where she stood stiffly facing Allie.

Allie shut the car door and leaned against her sport utility vehicle admiring the paint filly. Large patches of white splashed her black shoulders and flanks and blazed down her face. The filly's well-muscled shape and compact build showed why Zane thought she'd make a good stock horse. With her beautiful head, the filly was the kind of horse little girls fell in love with.

And big girls. To Allie, the colorful paint horses symbolized a mythical, magical, romantic Old West.

The paint maintained her vigilance, never taking her attention from Allie. Allie could read the fear and distrust in the filly's stance, in her stiff mouth, flared nostrils and wide-open eyes. The horse wanted to flee; the enclosed pen gave her nowhere to go.

Allie didn't need the increased flicking of the filly's ears to tell her Zane had walked up. She'd sensed him standing in the shadows of the barn's interior. Watching her. Before he spoke, she said, "A beauty like her, you'll have no trouble selling her. You don't need me to train her." Allie wanted to run as badly as the mare. Coming here had been a mistake.

"Selling her's not the problem."

The silence lengthened while Allie watched the filly. She wouldn't ask why he'd called. She wouldn't mention the past, his daughter or his wife. They had nothing to talk about. The only thing she wanted to say was goodbye. "What's wrong with her?" she blurted out and wanted to kick herself for showing interest.

"Some fool over near Rifle decided to play cowboy and raise quarterhorses. No one told him if two solid-colored horses each have a recessive overo gene, they could produce a paint foal with an overo-patterned coat. When he found out he couldn't register the filly as a quarterhorse because of her paint markings, he sold her for chicken-feed to a kid who'd never had a horse and didn't have a clue how to train one."

Allie refused to look at him. "I suppose he mistreated her." Dumb, dumb, dumb to prolong the conversation when Allie had no intention of helping with the filly.

"No, but he expected her to act like a ten-year-old trained mare, and when she didn't, he sold her to a spoiled teenage girl who thought the filly was cute and whipped her when she wasn't. The girl sold her to a man who bought the filly for his daughter and he turned her over to one of his hands who tried to break the filly through fear and punishment. When the owner told me about the paint, I thought she deserved another chance."

To a stranger, their conversation might sound normal, but Allie heard the tension in Zane's voice.

The filly watched them apprehensively. Experience had taught her humans couldn't be trusted. She didn't know she could trust Allie. Or Zane. No matter what Zane had done to Allie, he'd never abuse an animal. "You could train her," Allie said.

"You get her started and I'll finish her."

Her cue to refuse, but the filly's fear tugged at Allie's heart. The wrong approach could ruin the horse forever. Allie walked around her SUV to the driver's side. "She'll take time."

"Then you'll do it?"

"I'll see how it goes." The setting sun heated the side of her face. "With Cheyenne away, I'm running the agency by myself, so I'll have to schedule around work."

"I heard you resigned your teaching position." He paused. "Want me to bring in a horse for you tomorrow?"

"I'll bring Copper. Nothing spooks her."

"Would you like a cup of coffee? Some iced tea or lemonade?"

"No." Allie reached for the door handle. All she wanted was to escape.

He couldn't let her go. Not yet. Zane pushed against the car door, preventing her from opening it. There were so many things he wanted to say to her. About how much he'd missed her. How much he regretted hurting her. How much he loved her.

Afraid to say any of it, he said, "We've known each other a long time, Allie. Couldn't we at least try to be friends?"

"No." She directed a cool look at him. "I want to be able to trust my friends. Move your hand before you lose it."

"I'd give anything, my right arm if I could, if it would change what happened."

"How dramatic," she said lightly. "Hasn't anyone ever told you, you can't change the past?"

He wanted to smash through the thick wall she'd built around herself, but he didn't know how. "I didn't plan to hurt you." Her face dismissed his words for the inadequate excuse they were.

"I lived." She pushed at his arm to remove his hand from her car door.

Her touch sent a shock of longing through him. He wanted to explain. He wanted understanding. Forgiveness where forgiveness was impossible. He wanted her to love him. "Just listen to me." Zane plunged ahead before she could argue. "You told me to go away, said I was too much like your father. You said you'd never marry me." She'd sounded so adamant, he hadn't tried to dissuade her, but had stumbled to his truck and driven to the nearest bar.

"I was angry and hurt, and Kim listened to me. I didn't sleep with her to get back at you." Allie flung up her head, making no effort to hide her disbelief. "All right," Zane said savagely, "maybe I did. Maybe I wanted to prove to you that another woman wanted me in spite of all those flaws you'd enumerated at great length." He gave a bitter laugh. "Oh, I proved something, didn't I? I proved I was every bit as immature and irresponsible as you said I was.''

She didn't bother to disagree. Zane doggedly continued. ''No matter how juvenile my reasons for sleeping with Kim, she became pregnant with my child. I couldn't ignore the situation. I had to marry her.'' Despite what Allie believed, that was the first time he'd ever gotten drunk. The first and only. Although when he realized the bitter cost of his shameful behavior, he'd been tempted to drown his troubles in alcohol. ''It wouldn't have been fair to marry her and then refuse to try to make the marriage work. I hoped we could be comfortable together, raise our child. I intended it to be a real marriage.''

He held Allie's gaze. ''In every way.'' The way her eyes darkened told him she knew what he meant. He locked his hands on Allie's arms, forcing her to stay and listen. ''Our marriage was not a success.''

''I'm not interested.''

An urgent need to break through the barriers she'd erected compelled him to go where he knew he had no business going. ''Get interested. Ask me why our marriage didn't work.''

''I don't care why.''

His fingers tightened. ''Ask me,'' he ordered through clenched teeth.

This time he had no trouble reading her face. She wanted to tell him to go to hell. She wanted to ask.

She gave a long-suffering sigh. "All right. Why didn't your marriage work?"

Her patronizing voice filled him with fury. He was practically on his knees, and she wanted him to think she was humoring him. She couldn't quite carry off a contemptuous twist of her lips. Or disguise the heaving of her breast. Zane tossed common sense in the dirt. "This, is why."

She made an O of surprise with her mouth as he lifted her to her toes. He kissed her before she had a chance to argue. Her body went stiff as a fence post. He wanted to toss her down on the ground and rip that filthy shirt off her. He wanted to nuzzle her breasts and wrap her long legs around him. He wanted to touch her in a million and one ways and places. He allowed himself to touch nothing but her mouth and her arms.

Allie didn't respond, but she didn't pull away. His body hardened as he feasted on the fullness of her bottom lip. She hated her lower lip, thought it pouty. Loving it, he ran his tongue over it. When her mouth softened, he slid the tip of his tongue between her parted lips.

Her breathing quickened. She wasn't as disinterested as she pretended. Her body betrayed her arousal. Zane wondered how far he could go, and his body grew so tight at the thought he almost lost control.

Knowing she'd never forgive him if he did what he longed to do, Zane eased his grip and stepped back. His shallow, rapid breathing echoed hers. He didn't care if she noticed. "I think you get the picture."

Despite the pulse racing in her throat and the breathing she couldn't control, she tried to act cool and unaffected by his kiss. "I get the picture. You forced your kisses on your wife, and she didn't like them any better than I do." Allie's voice barely shook. "Do not kiss me again."

She deliberately misunderstood him. Just as she was deliberately ignoring her response to his kiss. Fighting her feelings and fighting him. He wanted to smile. Allie would go down fighting. He did smile at that. He liked a good fight.

When he won. His smile vanished.

He'd been stupid to risk everything by kissing her. He'd waited five years. He could have waited longer. Given her time.

If that much time existed.

He wanted to kiss her again. Instead he brushed her cheek with the back of his hand. "I won't kiss you again until you want to kiss me." The words he'd meant as compliance with her wishes echoed arrogantly.

Quick anger flashed in her eyes before they narrowed with cunning. "It's a deal. We won't kiss again until I want to kiss you." Taking his silence for agreement, Allie reached for the car door handle.

"Who's here, Daddy?"

Hannah's voice came from the direction of the house. Zane didn't take his eyes off Allie. "Allie Lassiter. The lady you met at the wedding."

"I wanna see Allie."

"I have to leave."

Zane held on to the door. "You can stay long enough to say hello to Hannah."

"I'm not interested in saying hello to your daughter."

Her cold, brittle voice cut like ground glass in his gut. He'd done this to her. Nothing he could do or say would ever change that fact. Or reach the depths of his regret. She'd agreed to help the filly. She would come to his ranch. He could see her. Talk to her. That would have to be enough.

Hannah skipped to his side. "Hi, Allie. How come you're here?"

"To see the paint," Allie answered curtly.

Zane smiled down at his ragamuffin of a daughter. She looked as bad as Allie in her dirty jeans and shirt. She'd lost another button. He'd be glad when she learned to do her own mending. Little needles and his big hands didn't go together.

"Isn't she beautiful? Daddy said she has to go to school. He said you're a teacher."

"I used to be. I don't teach anymore."

Red curls bobbed as Hannah nodded her head vigorously and pointed to the filly. "Daddy said you're gonna teach her. He promised."

Hannah had a habit of taking every word he said as a kind of pronouncement from on high. Zane smiled wryly at Allie.

She glared back. "Your father's good at making promises. He's not very good at keeping them."

Jamming her key into the ignition, Allie added in a tight voice, "I won't be back."

He couldn't believe it. Damn it, she'd been a teacher. She ought to know how kids interpreted things. She did know. Hannah's remarks had given her the excuse she wanted.

Zane wanted to throw back his head and howl in despair. Frustration and pain boiled up from deep inside him. Slamming her car door shut, Zane braced his hands on the rolled-down window and stuck his face close to hers.

"Does this make you feel better, Alberta? I betrayed you so you're refusing to help a blameless filly and rejecting a little girl who's reaching out to you for friendship. Do you think sinking to my level will make you feel better? I've got news for you, honey. Life down here in the slime pits is dark and dirty and rank, and you'll hate yourself from the moment you wake up in the morning until you work yourself into an exhausted sleep at night. And every time you look in a mirror, you'll loathe the person looking back at you."

"My, don't we feel sorry for ourselves? Why don't you have a beer and forget your troubles? It worked for you before."

Her words slashed painfully deep. Zane dropped his hands and stepped back. Allie's car roared into life and tore out of the ranch yard. The dust swirling around his boots smothered the false crumbs of hope he'd secretly nourished.

*   *   *

A car honked behind her. Allie checked her rear-view mirror as an unfamiliar car flashed around her. Her eyes darted back to the mirror and her own image. She looked no different. The same blue eyes, shaggy blond hair, chopped-off chin, ordinary nose. Only the mouth seemed different. As if it didn't belong to her. Because she didn't want to lay claim to a mouth that could say such horrible, hurtful words. The ugly taunt replayed itself endlessly in her mind.

Hateful words. Said in a reasonable, quiet tone of voice, which made them all the more hateful. "Proud of yourself, Alberta Lassiter?" she mocked her twin in the mirror. Worse was the shameful knowledge Zane had been right. She'd refused to help the filly because she didn't have the power to hurt Zane the way he'd hurt her.

Allie pulled over to the side of the road and parked. She'd always thought of herself as a good person. Condemning others for callous and uncaring behavior, she'd set herself up as a paragon of goodness and mercy. Prided herself on her compassion.

Closing her eyes, she leaned back against the headrest. She was a fraud, her behavior a total sham, her heart as black as three of the filly's legs.

She wanted to blame Zane Peters for pulling her down. "The slime pits," he'd said. "Dark and dirty and rank." He'd put himself there.

He couldn't put her there. Only she could.

Starting the engine, Allie retraced her route.

The paint filly had joined a small herd in a nearby

pasture. Zane stood by the corral watching the horses. His daughter sat on the top rail, leaning back against her father's chest. Allie forced her legs to carry her across the yard.

Zane didn't turn as Allie leaned on the corral beside him.

The child peeked around her father, then curled tighter into Zane. Her thumb sought her mouth.

"I apologize for what I said." For all Zane's response, Allie could have spoken a foreign language. "And I'm sorry I said it in front of your daughter."

Moments passed before Zane spoke. "I haven't had a drop of any kind of alcohol since that night."

"That's good." Allie drew on a rail with her finger. She knew he meant the night he'd impregnated Kim Taylor.

The sun took its warmth below the mountain peaks. Zane straightened, and lifting his daughter from the railing, settled her on his shoulders. "Thanks for coming back. I know how difficult it was for you to apologize, and I appreciate it." He turned toward the house.

Allie rubbed her palms along the seams of her jeans. He wasn't making this easy for her. "You don't need to put the filly in the round pen tomorrow. I'll bring her in."

Zane didn't slow his pace. "All right."

"All right? That's all you have to say?" she shouted after him.

He stopped. "What did you expect me to say?" he asked without turning.

"You could act a little surprised that I'm coming."

"I'm not surprised. I knew you'd come tomorrow."

She couldn't let it go. "I suppose you knew I'd come back tonight, too."

At that he turned. "Alberta, sometimes I think I know you better than I know myself."

"You don't know me at all. If you did, you'd know I hate to be called Alberta."

"I know you hate it." Sliding one hand up and down his daughter's denim-clad leg, Zane gave Allie a slow smile. "And, yes, Alberta, I knew you'd be back."

He took his daughter into the house leaving Allie standing there. She hated him. Hated his teasing, his smile, his little girl who wasn't hers. Hated his wide shoulders and lean hips. Hated that a mere flexing of facial muscles could jolt a person's stomach and speed up her heart.

Once that slow smile would have sent Allie rushing into Zane's open arms. Older and wiser, she knew the difference between love and shallow physical attraction. Besides, Zane no longer had open arms. His daughter filled his arms.

Her face had told Zane how close he'd come to ruining everything. His only excuse was giddy, overwhelming relief. He'd gambled, remembering how painfully honest with herself Allie had always been. He'd told himself she'd come back. Reminded himself she'd never walk away from an animal in need. He hadn't realized how scared he'd been until she'd returned.

Then he'd wanted to shout with joy and grab her in his arms.

The years, his marriage, Hannah—they changed nothing. He wanted Allie Lassiter. She'd stood there in ragged, dirty clothes—worn deliberately, he'd bet—her nose pointed snootily skyward, her eyes dark with annoyance, and Zane had wanted to send Hannah to the house and throw Allie down in the dirt and make mad, passionate love to her.

He had to be content with Allie's agreeing to come to the ranch and help the filly. The animal had enough problems to keep Allie coming for a long time.

But was it long enough for Zane to break through the fences she'd erected around herself? Fences for which he'd supplied the barbed wire and poles.

The reason he'd betrayed Allie came padding on bare feet down the stairs. "Daddy?"

No, he hadn't betrayed Allie because of Hannah. That he had a daughter was the result of his behavior, not the cause. He smiled at her. "Ready for a story before bed?"

Hannah crossed the room and eyed him solemnly. "How come Allie talked mean to us?"

"Allie didn't talk...well, I suppose it sounded that way to you." He scooped his daughter up on his lap. "Sometimes when people get hurt, they sound angry." Before Hannah could ask where

Allie hurt, Zane quickly steered the conversation away from Allie. "Remember when you stubbed your big toe on the footstool the other night?"

Hannah nodded. "It hurt really, really bad and I cried."

"You were grouchier than a hungry bear. You growled and growled, like this." Zane made growling sounds and pretended to bite her neck.

Hannah squirmed around until she faced him. "No, no! I growled like this." She roared at the top of her lungs.

Zane laughed and hugged her tightly, breathing in the smell of baby shampoo. Holding her close, he stood. "C'mon, little bear, time for your prayers and a story, then beddy-bye."

On the side of her bed, Hannah curled in his lap, squeezed her eyelids tightly shut and pressed her palms together. "Hi, Mommy. Daddy and I played bear."

Zane didn't know how Hannah's nightly prayers came to mean chatting with her mother, who was no one's idea of an angel or a saint. His book on how-to-parent hadn't covered how one explained to a toddler the death of the mother she'd barely known. Kim hadn't been much of a mother, but he hoped her daughter never learned that.

There was so much he hoped Hannah would never learn about. War and hate and pain and betrayal. Zane smoothed a hand over his daughter's soft, rumpled curls, knowing he couldn't protect her forever. Horses broke legs, dogs bit, kids at school said cruel things, animals and people you cared about died.

Heading the long list of bad things in the world were people who betrayed you. How did a parent protect a daughter from a man like him?

Mary Lassiter hadn't been able to protect Allie.

Copper greeted Worth with a nicker as he walked up to the horse trailer. Her brother scratched the crest of the elderly mare's mane and smiled at Allie. "Need any help?"

"If that's your subtle way of asking why I'm loading Copper and where I'm going with the horse trailer, I told Mom."

"Zane called this morning and told me you're going to help him with a horse."

Finished loading the mare, Allie gave Copper a pat on the rump and closed the back of the trailer. "I'm not helping him anything. I'm helping the filly." She stepped around the greyhound at her heels.

"Do you want to talk about it? I never knew what you and Zane fought about that night he went to the bar."

"What we always fought about. I felt he sometimes acted too much like Beau, irresponsible, not ready to settle down." Allie gave a bitter laugh. "I didn't know how close to the truth I was." She hadn't known then, or when Zane had come back two days later, an apologetic smile on his lips, a bunch of hothouse flowers in one hand, and her ring in the other. She'd accepted all three because she'd loved him and because she'd believed him when he promised to grow up.

Allie rubbed her bare finger. He'd neglected mentioning that he'd gone straight from their argument to a local bar where, to celebrate his liberation and to prove what a big boy he was, he'd gotten roaring drunk. He'd also neglected to mention the sympathetic bartender who'd taken him home to her bed.

"That was five years ago," Worth said. "Zane wasn't much more than a kid. A man can do a lot of growing up in five years. You have to admit, he took responsibility for his actions, and didn't look for the easy way out. Zane could have supported the child without marrying Kim."

Allie carefully placed her gear in the trailer's storage area. "Is that what you would have done?"

"No. I'd have married her. Nothing against Mom and Grandpa and their raising of us, but I resented Beau for being a father in name only. I'd never allow a kid of mine to grow up without me there."

She shrugged. "It's all water under the bridge. There's no going back."

Worth shook his head in amusement. "You sound like Yancy. Grandpa always said the situation didn't exist that couldn't be covered by a well-worn cliché."

"He was right." She reached for the door handle.

Worth beat her to it and opened the door. "Now that Zane's a widower, you two could try again."

He moved aside as Moonie slid around him and leaped into the SUV.

"Not interested," Allie said flatly, climbing behind the steering wheel.

Without comment Worth stepped back and waved her on her way.

Driving down the highway, Allie thought darkly about Worth's tendency to view his younger sisters as about ten years old. "He'd better not be planning on playing matchmaker," she said to the greyhound looking out of the passenger window. Moonie turned and lay down, his head resting on Allie's thigh. She stroked his head. "Who needs a man when she has a dog?" A gentle snore met her rhetorical question.

Males. You couldn't count on them for anything. Except to let you down. In all fairness, she had to exempt her grandfather and her brother from the category of worthless males. Beau always said Worth fit his name. A person could count on Worth.

Turning off the highway, Allie wished her brother hadn't brought up the past. No one could resurrect what had been—Allie corrected herself—what she'd thought had been between her and Zane. People didn't mourn a one-sided love affair. Especially if you'd been the stupid one in love.

Worth talked about the difficulty of Zane's choice. At least Zane made his choice. Allie had been given no choice.

She cringed to think how gullible she'd been. How she'd seen Zane's exemplary behavior in the weeks before their upcoming wedding as proof he'd matured. Now she knew he'd been feeling guilty because he'd slept with Kimberly Taylor.

Five years later Allie still didn't know if she would have accepted back the ring if she'd known he'd slept with another woman. She told herself she wouldn't have, but she'd been young. And in love. The question would never be answered.

An aspen tree, its leaves gleaming with gold, caught her eye. The aspens had been green then, the green of spring and promise. She'd been sitting on the porch waiting for Zane, her mind jumbled with last-minute wedding plans. The memory of his face, pale with eyes almost black as he told her, superimposed itself on the ribbon of highway ahead of her.

"I slept with another woman. Kimberly Taylor. She's pregnant, Allie, so I'm going to marry her."

Her ears heard the words, but her mind refused to take in their meaning. "What do you mean? How? When? What are you talking about?"

Zane held his arms down stiffly in front of him, his hands gripping the wide brim of his hat. "I got drunk and slept with her the night you broke our engagement. She's pregnant."

"I don't believe you." She hadn't wanted to believe.

"I wish I were lying. I'm more sorry than I can say, Allie. I know this is a rotten thing to do to you."

Her throat had swollen, making it painful to swallow. "You're going to marry someone else?"

"I've thought about it and thought about it, but it's the right thing, the only thing, I can do. I was wrong to sleep with Kim, but I can't erase what I did. And now I have to do the honorable thing and marry her."

"What about me?" she'd cried.

He wouldn't look at her. Just stood there, curling his hat brim tighter and tighter. Finally he said, "You'll find someone else. A better man. A man who deserves you." He'd turned and walked toward his pickup.

She'd screamed at him then. Called him names, cursed him, heaped upon him every bit of verbal abuse that came to mind. Zane had stood by his truck, his hand on the door handle, his head bowed. Not until she'd run out of words had he picked up the ring she'd thrown in the dirt at his feet, climbed wearily into his truck and driven slowly away.

He'd married Kimberly Taylor the next day.

Zane Peters married or Zane Peters a widower, it was all the same to Allie. The filly drew her to his ranch. Not Zane.

And definitely not his daughter with her mother's hair. Allie should have guessed the girl's identity the minute she saw her. Despite her red hair, the child looked like Zane.

The gossip about Kim Taylor had quickly reached Allie. People seemed to think a jilted bride would be happy to know the man who'd jilted her was himself being cheated on. She hadn't been happy. The gossip only proved how little wrecking Allie's life meant to either Zane or Kim.

The child was swinging on a rope swing tied to a large cottonwood tree near the house when Allie drove up. At the sight of Allie's car and trailer, the little girl dragged her feet in the dirt, slowing down the swing.

Allie intended to concentrate on the filly, not on some other woman's kid. Ignoring the child, Allie opened the trailer and backed Copper down the short ramp.

"Hi."

"Hello," Allie answered shortly. So much for hoping the kid would stay out of her way.

"Daddy said I can't bother you."

"He's right."

"What's her name?"

Allie glanced over to see the girl petting the greyhound. "Moonie. You shouldn't pet strange dogs. You could get bitten."

"She likes me."

"He. He's a male dog." Males had no discrimination.

"He's funny-looking. He's skinny."

Telling Moonie to stay by the trailer, Allie swung up on Copper and walked the mare toward the pasture.

On short, stubby legs, the little girl trotted beside the large mare. "What's your horse's name? My new horse is Honey. Daddy calls me honey."

Allie carefully closed and locked the gate into the pasture. Zane's daughter said the endearment in exact mimicry of the way her father used to say it to Allie.

The child climbed up the metal pasture gate and clung to the top. "He calls me honey 'cuz he really loves me. I really love Honey."

Allie wheeled Copper around and gave the small girl a stern look. "Your father told you not to bother me. Go back to your swing and stay there." Allie refused to call the paint Honey.

The filly stood in the middle of a group of horses. As Allie guided Copper slowly toward the small herd, a brown mare nickered a greeting to Copper, and Allie's mare nickered back. Used to horses with riders, the horses curiously watched Allie's approach. Their calm behavior reassured the filly. Slowly Allie guided the small herd toward the open gate of the round pen. The horses obligingly ambled inside.

One by one, Allie extracted the horses from the pen until only the paint remained. Paying no attention to the filly, Allie shut the gate, then guided Copper around the pen, walking at first, then trotting. All the while, Allie talked in a low, calm voice. Eventually the filly, curious or wanting to herd up with Copper, trotted in their wake. Allie gradually slowed her mare until the filly moved almost abreast of them. Now she patted and rubbed Copper, her hand coming closer by degrees to the paint but never touching the filly. At first the filly shied away each time Allie's hand moved, but imperceptibly she grew accustomed to the movement.

Round and round. Finally Allie guided Copper over to the gate. When she opened the gate, the filly humped her back at the noise, but quickly spotted the opening and dashed into the pasture. After a few yards, she slowed and turned to look at Allie. "That wasn't so bad, was it?" Allie asked.

"You have more patience than any woman I know, and you hardly ever lose your temper. I'll bet you made a good school teacher."

Focused on the filly, Allie had missed Zane's approach. She rode Copper through the pasture gate Zane held open and guided the mare toward the horse trailer. "Hardly ever," he'd said.

She knew he referred to the night she'd totally lost control, screaming and yelling like a banshee. "I never claimed to be a saint," she said. "If you'd wanted a submissive namby-pamby, you shouldn't have gotten engaged to me in the first place."

Zane raised an eyebrow. "Where'd that come from? I was complimenting you."

He knew very well what she was talking about. Allie pushed him aside when he would have removed Copper's saddle. "I take care of my own horse, and I don't want your compliments. I don't want you checking up on me. If you don't trust me with the filly, train her yourself."

"I'm not checking up. I wanted to talk to you."

"We have nothing to talk about."

He leaned against the side of the trailer. "We

haven't discussed what it's going to cost me for you to work with the filly.''

Everything, she wanted to scream. He owed her for more than a few minutes a day training a horse. He could never repay her for what he owed her. ''I'm not training the filly for you.''

Zane gave her a crooked smile. ''I don't think Hannah's allowance will cover horse-training.''

She turned away, fussing with Copper. It wasn't fair that a smile from a low-down skunk could unsettle her stomach and interfere with her breathing. Against the mare's flank, she muttered, ''I'm here for the filly's sake. No other reason.''

He didn't reply. Crossed at the ankles, his worn boots remained in her field of vision. Hardworking, serviceable boots. If they'd ever seen a lick of polish, it didn't show. She wished he'd take them out of her sight.

He uncrossed his ankles. ''You're making Hannah happy.''

''Your daughter's your responsibility, not mine.''

''Hannah's not a responsibility. She's a privilege and a joy.''

Allie put Copper in the trailer, glad the task kept her face from Zane's view. Once she'd anticipated having his children. Dreamed of seeing her sons and daughters on his shoulders, on his lap, in his arms. Her Hannah. Not another woman's. Allie settled her hat firmly on her head, jumped down from the trailer and latched the back. ''I should be able to come tomorrow. You told your daughter not to bother me. Take your own advice.''

Zane looked around. ''Where is Hannah? I'm surprised the temptation of watching you and the filly wasn't too much for her. Ruth must have called her in for dinner.'' He hesitated, then walked toward the house.

Guilt needled Allie as she thought of her stern directive to the little girl. Not that she'd been wrong to order the child away from the corral. The girl would have disturbed Allie's concentration and distracted the filly. Allie had no reason to feel guilty about a rational decision. Maybe Zane's daughter had looked a little down at the mouth, but she was obviously a spoiled brat who used tears and pouting to wrap her father around her finger. Spoiling a child was bad for her. The child had to learn she couldn't always do what she wanted.

Allie looked around for Moonie, frowning. It wasn't like the greyhound to leave the spot where he'd been told to stay. Failing to locate him, she called, ''Moonie, come here, boy, come. We're going home, boy. Home!''

A sharp bark answered her call. Looking in the direction of the sound, Allie saw Moonie standing at the base of the large cottonwood tree.

''Come on, boy. Let's go.''

The dog barked urgently, but stayed where he was.

Irritation swept over Allie. If that kid had dragged Moonie over there and tied him to the tree and then gone off and left him... Allie stomped toward the tree.

Stiff-legged, Moonie raised the pitch of his barking.

Seeing a patch of blue beside the dog, Allie broke into a run.

Zane's daughter lay in a heap beneath the rope swing. Tears mingled with dirt to smear mud over her cheeks. "My arm hurts," she whimpered as Allie dropped to her knees beside the child.

"Hannah?" Zane called from the front of the house.

"She's over here. She hurt her arm," Allie added as Zane came around the corner.

Trying to avoid bumping the arm his daughter cradled with her other hand, Zane carefully lifted her into his arms. "It's okay, honey, Daddy has you. What happened?"

"I went really high to watch Allie and Honey and I fell." She gave him a tiny, waterlogged smile of triumph. "I'm a good girl, Daddy. I stayed at my swing like Allie told me."

CHAPTER THREE

ALLIE'S stomach churned with guilt and self-condemnation. Zane hadn't given her a single accusatory look. He hadn't uttered one word of blame. He hadn't yelled at her for ordering his daughter to stay on the swing. He hadn't blamed his daughter's accident on Allie or done or said anything indicating he thought Allie was in any way at fault.

He didn't have to. Allie knew she was to blame.

Greeley walked into the hospital waiting room in Aspen. "How is she?"

"She broke her left radius. This bone." Allie pointed to her lower arm. "Luckily it was a simple fracture. They didn't have to move it back into place or anything. They're putting on a cast now. What are you doing here?"

"After you called her, Mom called me on the cell phone since I was on my way to Aspen to deliver a sculpture. I picked up Moonie from Zane's truck and went over to your place and fed Amber and Moonie and walked him. He refused to stay there, so he's out in my truck." Greeley sat beside Allie. "Mom said you sounded pretty upset. You okay?"

"Sure, why wouldn't I be? I didn't break anything. It was all my fault," Allie added in a rush.

"You push her out of the swing?"

Greeley meant the question to be absurd, but her sister wasn't so far wrong. "I sent her away. Told her to go to her swing and stay there. When she fell, she lay under the swing in pain. She told Zane she was being a good girl."

"Don't tell me Zane is blaming you."

"He hasn't said anything, but he must blame me. If I hadn't told her to stay there…"

"It could have been dangerous for you or for her if she'd climbed up on the round pen while you were working a green filly. You did the right thing telling her to stay away."

"I shouldn't have spoken so harshly."

"Harshly? Or firmly?"

Allie clenched her hands together. "I used the voice I use when boys are fighting on the playground. Worth calls it my 'or else' voice."

"An adult has to protect children from themselves. Don't make a mountain out of a molehill."

Allie didn't know what to do with her hands. She picked at the frayed edges of the hole in the knee of her jeans. "I never wanted her to get hurt. I didn't mean…"

Greeley patted Allie's restless fingers. "Of course you didn't."

"Didn't I?" The words burst from Allie. "What if, subconsciously, I wanted to hurt her, wanted her to go away, not just from the round pen, but go away forever?''

"What is with you? You don't usually dramatize like this.''

"I'm serious, Greeley. I've been sitting here thinking about how much Zane hurt me and how much I hated him and hated that woman he married.''

"What does all this have to do with the girl's fall?''

"Don't you get it?'' Allie leaned her head against the wall behind her chair. "The only reason Zane married that woman was because she was pregnant with his child. You have no idea how much I resented one little girl. It's unreasonable, childish and ugly, but I couldn't stop. I told myself she didn't ask to be born, but...'' Her voice faltered. "I couldn't stop thinking, if she hadn't been conceived, hadn't been born...''

"I don't think any of us had any idea you felt this way,'' Greeley said slowly. "Why didn't you say something?''

"What could I say that didn't make me out more of a fool than I'd already been? I'd loved Zane so much for so long. What does that say about me that I loved someone so worthless, someone who could hurt me so badly? I know what happened was Zane's fault, but if I blamed him, I admitted I was stupid, a loser. You know I'm too vain for that.'' Allie made a pathetic attempt at a smile. "But I had to blame someone, so I blamed the woman he married, and by extension the baby, because without the baby he never would have married that woman. None of it makes sense, but I couldn't help it.''

Greeley reached for Allie's hand and squeezed hard. "Listen to me, Allie Lassiter. Zane Peters's behavior does not reflect on you. Do you think Mom was stupid for putting up with Beau?''

Allie looked directly at her sister. "Yes.''

Greeley made a face. "Actually, so do I, so that was a bad example. Mom took him in every time he showed up at her door, knowing full well the second he healed enough, he'd cheat on her again. It's not the same at all with you and Zane.''

Her sister had missed the point. "Mom never seemed to resent you because of Beau sleeping with the woman who gave birth to you.''

"Mom knew what Beau and that woman did had nothing to do with me. Sometimes I thought she had to be pretending she loved me as much as she loved the rest of you.'' After a moment, she added, "I used to test her.''

"I know.'' Allie closed her eyes in despair. "I wish I were more like Mom. All I could think about was how Zane's daughter messed up my whole life. She's a baby, and I resented her. Greeley, I hated her.''

This evening when she'd found the child lying in pain beneath the swing, for the first time Allie had seen Hannah as an individual, not an extension of her mother or the reason why Zane had abandoned Allie. She'd wanted to take Hannah in her arms and hold her close, begging the child's forgiveness. The realization that she'd sunk so low as to hate a child appalled and shamed Allie. "I couldn't stand being around Hannah," she said in a tortured voice. "I couldn't even say her name. I couldn't bear talking to her or looking at her."

"You won't have to ever again. I'll find someone else to work with the filly."

Allie's eyes snapped open, and her stomach plunged to the floor. Zane had heard her confession to Greeley. The hard, angry look on his face told her he'd accept neither an apology nor an explanation. If one could explain the pain and confusion leading to such unforgivable behavior. Allie stared helplessly at him.

"Don't go off half-cocked, Zane," Greeley said. "Everyone's a little upset right now, but the important thing is, your daughter is all right. She is, isn't she? Where is Hannah?"

"The nurse took her to the bathroom so I could come talk to Allie. I was fool enough to think she might be concerned," Zane said in a clipped voice, his cold eyes never leaving Allie.

"Here we are." The nurse's voice rang cheerfully as she brought Hannah into the waiting room.

Thanking the nurse, Zane gathered up his daughter.

"Look, Allie, the doctor gave me a cast." Hannah's mouth turned down. "My arm hurts."

Allie felt sick. "I'm sorry," she said inadequately to the child.

Zane's upper lip curled with contempt, then softened as he looked away from Allie to his daughter. "Let's go home, honey."

"You said I get an ice-cream cone. Allie, too." Hannah looked at Greeley. "Who are you?"

"I'm Allie's sister. My name is Greeley."

"You want ice cream?"

"No, thanks. Moonie can have my cone."

"Daddy, Moonie eats ice cream."

Allie looked at Greeley in panic as her sister turned toward the door. "You have to give me a ride to Zane's place. I left the rig and put Copper in his corral so I could drive his truck while he took care of Hannah."

"I'll take you back," Zane said shortly. "No point in Greeley driving out there, when I'm going that way."

Allie took a deep breath. "You're right." She'd already delayed her sister. "Thanks, Greeley, for taking care of Amber and Moonie." At Greeley's doubtful look, Allie nodded. She didn't want to go with Zane any more than he wanted to take her, but shut in the truck with her, Zane would have to listen.

Moonie went crazy when he saw them come out of the hospital. Greeley opened her truck door and the greyhound shot out.

"The dog's not going with us," Zane said.

"I want Moonie," Hannah cried. "He's my friend."

"He won't hurt her. He's very gentle." Allie mo-

tioned to the dog to sit. Moonie's quivering tail reg-
istered his excitement as he obeyed.

Zane buckled Hannah into her child seat in the
back seat of his pickup. When he straightened,
Hannah said, "I want Moonie."

Allie released Moonie and the dog leaped into
Zane's truck and lay down, his muzzle on Hannah's
leg.

Zane frowned. "Put him up front with you."

"I want Moonie."

"Maybe he'll take her mind off her arm," Allie
said.

Zane gave Allie a scorching look but said no
more about the dog. They'd barely turned onto the
highway before Hannah fell asleep, slumping down
in her child seat, one hand resting on Moonie. The
greyhound lay perfectly still.

Facing forward, Allie spoke to the windshield.
"She's sound asleep. I think ice cream will have to
wait until another day."

Not bothering to acknowledge her words, Zane
made a U-turn near the Castle Creek bridge and
headed away from Aspen.

She had to do it now. Taking a deep breath, Allie
said, "What you heard back there, I'd like—"

"I'm not interested. When we get to my place,
pack up your dog and your horse and leave. If you
see me on the street, don't bother to say hello. I'll
return the favor."

"If you'd let me explain." Reaching over, she
touched his arm.

He flinched at her touch, jerked the wheel, then, swearing, brought the large pickup under control. A few minutes later, he said tight-jawed, "Don't touch me, and don't say another word, or so help me, you'll walk the rest of the way. Just shut up."

His stubborn refusal to listen angered her. "I am not going to shut up, and you're not dumping me anywhere. You dumped me for the last time when you dumped me just before our wedding. You owe me the courtesy of listening to what I have to say."

"Fine. Talk. Get it out of your system."

"I don't know how much you heard me say at the hospital."

"Enough to know you're blaming an innocent kid. Damn it, Allie, my daughter had nothing to do with what happened. How could you hold the circumstances of her birth against her?"

"How could you do what you did to me?" she flashed.

"It comes back to that, doesn't it?"

Chilled, Allie pulled her jacket tighter. "This isn't about us," she said, keeping her voice low. "It's about your daughter. I'm ashamed I resented, okay, hated, a child I didn't even know. This afternoon, when Hannah was so proud of herself for being good..." Allie bit her lip and looked out the window into the black night. After a minute, she went on, "She looked so little and was so brave..." Allie cleared her throat. "Things I've thought and said... They're inexcusable, and there's probably nothing I can say to convince you, but I'm truly sorry about what happened to Hannah.''

Eventually Allie gave up waiting for Zane to respond to her apology. She couldn't fault him for his anger. She'd said horrible, nasty things. He couldn't hate the way she'd behaved more than she hated it. How could she focus all her hurt and anger on one small child? If only she could convince herself she hadn't subconsciously hoped Hannah would somehow disappear.

Hannah's mother had died. Allie hadn't returned to Aspen for the funeral. She'd never asked if any of her family had attended Kim's funeral. Now she wondered if she'd subconsciously rejoiced. Perhaps found vindication in Kim Taylor's death. The unanswerable questions ricocheted painfully inside her skull.

Suppressing a sigh, Allie stared out the window. Fast-moving clumps of indigo-edged clouds played tag with early stars. She and Zane used to lie in a pasture and gaze at the heavens while he tried to teach her the names of some of the stars and constellations. He'd never taught her much more than the North Star and the Big Dipper because he would kiss her.

His lips had been warm and exciting.

Surreptitiously she studied his profile. She knew every inch of his rough-hewn jaw. Knew how it felt to slide her tongue down the slight depression running the length of his chin. Knew the unique flavor of his skin. Allie's eyes closed as memories threatened to overwhelm her. Five years had passed, and she remembered the taste and feel of his mouth as intimately and surely as if he'd kissed her five minutes ago.

Zane braked his truck in front of his house. "Hell," he said, hitting the steering wheel with his palms. "Not now."

Following his gaze, Allie saw an unfamiliar sedan parked to one side. "Company?"

"Not exactly." After a long moment, he took a deep breath and opened the truck's door. "Wake up, honey, we're home."

Allie jumped from the truck and hurried to the house to open the door for Zane. Moonie streaked by her into Zane's house.

"Get away from me! Vern! Get him away! Vern!"

The shrieks came from the house as Zane carefully carried Hannah inside. Allie followed him in to retrieve Moonie.

The greyhound sat on his haunches, his head cocked to one side as he stared curiously at the large woman standing precariously on the sofa above him. The woman made shooing motions at him.

"I'm sorry he alarmed you," Allie said, "but he won't hurt you. He's very friendly. Moonie, come here."

Giving the woman one last incredulous look, the greyhound trotted to Allie's side.

"A big dog like that ought to be on a rope." The

woman scowled at Allie as she stepped down. "Who are you?"

"Allie Lassiter." Realizing Moonie had frightened Zane's guest, Allie made allowances for the woman's behavior.

Dismissing Allie with a sniff, the woman turned to Zane, saw Hannah's arm and shrieked, "Did that mean dog bite my baby?"

"I broke my arm, Grandma Taylor," Hannah said proudly.

This rude, overweight woman was the mother of Zane's wife?

"Aren't you going to introduce me?" his mother-in-law asked peevishly.

"Allie," Zane said woodenly, "this is Edie Taylor."

Before Allie could respond, a heavyset man came from the back of the house, brushing off his shirt-front. "Whatcha yelling about? Ruthie doesn't know anything." Seeing Zane, he stopped. "Where the hell you been?"

"I broke my arm, Grandpa Taylor."

"Hello, Vern. Nice to see you again."

Allie heard the sarcasm in Zane's voice. Apparently no else did.

"Didn't you hear me hollering at you, Vern? I swear, you're getting deafer every day. The damned dog could have eaten me alive, and you'd be out in the kitchen feeding your face."

"Now, Edie, I couldn't help it if Ruthie insisted I have a piece of her special carrot cake, could I?"

"Tell him what we came for."

"I know what you came for," Zane said, "and you can forget it. A child belongs with her father."

Kim's parents wanted Hannah? Allie saw Hannah curl tighter into her father's arms, her wide eyes darting from her father to her grandparents and back. The child obviously sensed the tension in the room. Allie's heart ached for the little girl. Hannah's grandparents should know when a child lost her mother, she immediately worried her father would also disappear. Hannah needed Zane.

"Vern's got something to say about that," Edie Taylor said.

"He'll have to wait. Hannah hasn't had her dinner." Zane carried his daughter to the back of the house.

The Taylors sat side by side on the sofa, their postures making it clear they weren't leaving until they had their say.

Allie had no business staying. Hannah's maternal grandparents were none of her concern. She would have left if either Vern or Edie Taylor had exhibited one bit of genuine concern over Hannah's broken arm. Neither grandparent had made a move to kiss or hug their granddaughter. Whatever was going on between Zane and Kim's parents, Allie vowed to ensure Hannah's needs came first. She owed the child that much. Moonie obeyed her signal to go to the corner and lie down.

Zane returned to the living room. "Ruth's giving her something to eat." He took in Allie's presence with only a slight narrowing of his eyes. "I'm telling you this for the last time, Edie. Hannah is my daughter and she's staying with me."

"It's too far away out here," Edie said. "She needs to be in a city where she can go to school."

"She's too young for school," Zane said.

Edie folded her arms across her ample chest. "There's no reason we can't act like civilized people about this. We're just thinking of her. My baby needs a mother, and since she doesn't have one, a grandmother is the next best thing. If you loved her half as much as you say you do, you'd give her to me to raise."

"I appreciate your concern," Zane said evenly, "but Hannah stays with me."

"You can't take care of the kid by yourself," Vern said.

"I have Ruth."

"Ruth." Edie snorted. "She's not good for much."

"Now, Edie," her husband said, "Ruthie makes a hell of a good carrot cake."

"Ruth takes excellent care of Hannah," Zane said.

"My poor baby broke her arm." Edie made a show of wiping her eyes. "I can't imagine how that happened."

"Doesn't look to me like anybody pays attention to her," Vern added.

"She fell out of a swing," Zane said.

"That's what you say. We know how mean you treated Kim," Edie snapped.

"I've told you before, I'm not going to discuss my marriage with you, and Hannah stays with me. The subject is closed."

"Not by a long shot it isn't closed. Tell him, Vern."

"Found us a better lawyer. He said it isn't right you got everything when Kim died just because she never wrote a will. She should have left us something."

"I told you to take anything of Kim's you wanted and I gave you the money in her bank account."

"It wasn't much for a gal married to one of the biggest ranchers in this area," Vern sneered. "Some clothes and geegaws and a couple thousand dollars."

"Kim didn't believe in saving for a rainy day," Zane said.

"She said you were stingy. We told her to divorce you. The courts would have made you pay. Guess it was lucky for you she got killed when she did," Edie added spitefully. Her eyes glinted. "Maybe she did tell you she was going to leave and take the kid. Maybe Vern and I ought to hire a private detective to check on that so-called accident."

Allie had never heard a whisper of suspicion about Kim Taylor's death. Zane's wife had been killed when she barreled through a stop sign on a country road and a cattle truck hit her pickup. She might have survived if she'd been wearing a seat belt. Few survived a three-quarter-ton pickup rolling over them.

"It's your money," Zane said.

"Damn right it is. Tell him, Vern."

"Lawyer said we could get custody of the kid."

Edie Taylor gave Zane a triumphant smile. "Kim said things. We know what went on. And now the kid broke her arm. A judge will see things our way, believe you me."

"I'm her father. Hannah's staying with me."

Allie heard the tension in Zane's voice. Just as she'd seen the look on his face when Edie Taylor made her sly remark about knowing what had gone on. Allie couldn't imagine what Edie Taylor meant. Zane would never harm a woman, yet he clearly knew what the older woman referred to.

"Don't be an idiot, Peters," Vern said. "It isn't like you're planning to marry and give the kid a mother."

Allie gave Vern Taylor a startled look. Mary Lassiter said answers could be found in the most unexpected places if a person paid attention. Allie remembered being not much older than Hannah and wondering when her mother would walk out the door and not come back. As her father had done. With a few simple words, Allie could make up for the terrible thoughts she'd harbored against Hannah. She wouldn't cross the road for Zane, but she'd do this for Hannah. The child needed her father.

Moving to Zane's side, Allie laid her hand lightly on his arm. "I think we should tell the Taylors our news. As Hannah's grandparents they're naturally concerned about her well-being."

Zane studied Allie's fixed smile. "You tell them."

"All right." At times like this, a woman needed the ability to blush at will. Lacking that, Allie gave the Taylors a coy smile and said, "Zane and I are planning to get married." Beneath her hand, a muscle twitched violently in Zane's arm.

"Married!" Edie and Vern said in shrill unison.

"You never said anything about getting married," Edie added accusingly.

"We decided tonight on the way home from the hospital," Allie said. "As you pointed out, Mrs. Taylor, Zane needs a mother for Hannah."

"You always claim you're so busy working," Edie said belligerently to Zane, "how'd you have time to meet some woman?"

"Our families have been friends for years," Allie quickly answered. "Zane and I hadn't seen each other for ages, and when we met recently at my sister's wedding, well..." She managed to give Zane a loving glance.

He gazed thoughtfully back. "Now that's out in the open, let's go eat with Hannah. I'm starving."

"When are you getting married?" Edie wanted to know.

"We haven't planned that far ahead," Allie said hurriedly.

A crooked smile bent Zane's mouth. "Now,

Allie,'' he drawled, ''we can tell Edie and Vern. The wedding's Monday.''

Allie goggled at him. Didn't he realize the only reason she said they planned to marry was to give him time to figure out how to deal with the Taylors' threats? She had no intention of actually marrying him.

''I don't know why you have to rush into it,'' Edie said petulantly. ''She pregnant, too?''

Allie opened her mouth.

Zane beat her into speech. ''We're madly in love.''

Allie wanted to kick his sarcastic shin.

''Allie doesn't want to burden her mom with a large wedding right after Mary put on a big shindig for her oldest daughter,'' Zane continued. ''It'll be just family. You're invited, of course. I'll phone you with the details when we get them hammered out.''

There was going to be some hammering all right. But not of details. Allie intended to hammer Zane's head. When they didn't get married on Monday, the Taylors would know Allie's announcement had been a hoax and they'd use that as further ammunition to gain custody of Hannah. What had happened to Zane's brains? He used to think as fast on his feet as Worth.

''We're busy,'' Edie said rudely. ''Come on, Vern.''

''One moment.'' Zane's cold voice would have frozen an icebreaker in place. ''Allie is not pregnant, but even if she were, it would be none of your business. You say so much as one lying word about her to anyone, and it will get back to me, and you'll find the welcome mat here yanked out from under you, grandparents or not. Do I make myself clear?''

They slammed the door behind them.

Allie momentarily forgot her own grievance. ''What kind of grandparents are they? They didn't even bother to tell Hannah goodbye. No judge in his right mind would award them custody.''

Which brought her back to Hannah's father. ''What was all that nonsense about getting married on Monday? You know very well we aren't—''

''Supper first,'' Zane smoothly interrupted. ''Ruth will have fixed plenty. After I get my poor, little, injured baby tucked in for the night, we can talk.''

Injured. And whose fault was that? A queasy feeling that had nothing to do with hunger settled heavily in Allie's stomach as she followed Zane to the kitchen.

Allie went downstairs, leaving Zane to tuck his daughter into bed. Hannah had insisted Allie accompany her and her father upstairs. Allie had agreed, suspecting the little girl, with one arm in a cast, would need extra help, but Zane had proven up to the challenge, handling the bedtime rituals with the ease that comes through practice.

Sitting on the sofa, automatically petting Moonie when he stuck his head in her lap, Allie surveyed Zane's living room. She hadn't been in this house for five years, but nothing had changed. Kim Taylor had altered the course of Zane's and Allie's lives and given birth to a daughter, but she'd left no discernible mark on the house where she'd spent her short married life. Familiar furniture filled the room. The same pictures hung on the wall.

Only one thing had changed. Allie no longer expected to live the rest of her life here.

Moonie lifted his head.

"Thanks for seeing her to bed. I apologize for her behavior at the table." Zane dropped into a worn brown leather chair. "She's usually a pretty good kid."

"Her arm hurt and dinner was too late for her."

"I try not to spoil her, but I probably let her have her own way too often. Edie's right. She needs a mom."

"No."

"All kids need a mom."

"No, I'm not marrying you the day after tomorrow, I don't care if you're raising a dozen motherless children."

Zane nodded toward Moonie. "I suppose he's one of those rescued greyhounds people adopt so they don't get put down. Was he too slow or too old?"

"Too slow. You said we'd discuss after dinner what you told your in-laws, so talk."

"We're talking. How's that black lab, what was his name? Shadow? The one you begged Worth to let you keep when he showed up at the Double

Nickel nothing but skin and bones with a poorly healed broken hip."

"He's old. Hard of hearing and almost deaf, but he gets around okay, even if he does spend most of the day lying in the sun. If you don't want to talk about this, fine with me. I have nothing to say, other than I'm not going to marry you."

Zane leaned his head back and closed his eyes. "I could have sworn you told Edie and Vern you were."

He looked worn-out. She didn't care. "The only reason I said we were getting married was to throw a monkey wrench in the Taylors' plans, and you know it."

"Have you ever refused to help an animal in trouble?"

"You're not an animal in trouble."

"Shadow. This skinny excuse for a dog." He petted Moonie who'd made his way to lean against Zane's leg. "The paint filly. Countless others, helpless creatures. Like Hannah."

Ignoring a twitch of pity, Allie said firmly, "Hannah isn't helpless. She has you."

"I'll do anything to keep her out of their hands."

He spoke quietly, but Allie had no doubt he meant what he said. "Why do they want Hannah? They don't seem to care much about her."

"They don't give a damn about her." He opened his eyes to give Allie a mocking look. "You shouldn't have been so quick to oppose them. They hate me almost as much as you do."

"Why? Did you betray them, too?" The slightest tightening of his lips told her her spiteful question hit its target.

"They thought Kim's marrying me was their winning lottery ticket. They constantly hounded her for money, and when she died, the spigot went dry. They wanted more, and I couldn't see any reason to give it to them."

"What's that got to do with Hannah?"

"Child support. Money to spend and no one to prove whether or not it's spent on Hannah."

"Surely not," Allie said, repelled.

"You think everyone grew up like you?" Zane asked harshly.

As a teacher she knew such things happened, but she'd never understood the way people could hurt children in a custody battle. "No, but they're her grandparents."

"You had a stable home, a loving mother, warm clothes, plenty of food on the table and money for extras. Your mom gave you direction, expected your best from you. Kim lived a hardscrabble life with parents who didn't give a damn if she made good grades or even went to school or ate breakfast or had a dress for a dance. That's not going to happen to Hannah."

Allie hardened her heart against the bleak look on Zane's face. "Nobody's going to take Hannah away from you."

"Nobody's going to get the chance. You told

Edie and Vern we're getting married, and I'm holding you to it.''

"Don't be ridiculous. Even if I did open my mouth and say something stupid, you're the one who blurted out the wedding is supposed to be the day after tomorrow. We could have dragged out a mythical engagement for years and then said we changed our minds.''

"You don't know Edie. Once you opened your mouth, we'd have had to get married sooner or later, or she'd have schemed until she figured out a way to use your announcement against me.''

"You can't make me feel guilty, and you have no right to ask me to come to your rescue.''

"I'm not asking you to come to my rescue. I'm asking you to come to Hannah's.'' His mouth twisted. "Or was that sniveling apology in the pickup just so many words, when the truth is you still hate Hannah because she's Kim's and my daughter?''

"I do not hate her, and you can't use my stupid words to force me into marrying you.''

"Daddy.'' Hannah stood in the doorway, tears dripping down her face. "My arm hurts. I don't like falling out of swings.''

CHAPTER FOUR

IF IT had been possible to obtain a marriage license, Zane would have married her tonight, but the license place was closed until Monday. Married to Allie. Zane crossed his arms beneath his head and treasured the memory of the look on Allie's face when Hannah had appeared. If he'd coached his daughter, she couldn't have timed her arrival better.

Whatever Allie had intended by her outrageous announcement, marrying him wasn't it. She said she meant to get his in-laws off his back, at least for the time being. The Taylors didn't worry him. Nor did their vague accusations that he'd mistreated his wife. Lies couldn't hurt him.

As for the guilt, Zane had learned to live with it. He'd tried to make his marriage work, determined to give Kim his loyalty as well as his name. It hadn't been enough for her.

Zane wondered how Allie would react if he told her she couldn't begin to hate Kim as much as Kim had hated Allie. Not once had he mentioned Allie's name to Kim, but his wife knew about the engagement. And knew, though neither of them ever spoke of it, Zane had never stopped loving Allie.

He could no more stop loving Allie than he could stop the sun from rising.

He stared at the ceiling, glad there were no mirrors up there. The great lover. He'd had sex with one woman and messed up the lives of three people. Four, if he counted Hannah.

Heaven help him if the Taylors ever figured out he'd pay to keep Hannah. If they suspected...no, Edie was fishing. One thing he knew about his esteemed former mother-in-law was that if she knew anything, she'd have used it against him by now. Edie and Vern had been sniffing around since Kim died, in an effort to find something they could use as a lever to pry money out of him. They'd found nothing. He told himself, there was nothing.

He wasn't desperate enough to marry Allie to keep Hannah.

He wanted to marry Allie for entirely different reasons.

They weren't married yet. Hannah might have turned the trick tonight, but Allie would have second thoughts. He'd picked the earliest possible day they could be married so Allie wouldn't have too much time to think. He didn't want her thinking.

He wanted her making love with him.

Zane slid a hand across the empty space at his side, then realizing what he was doing, stopped, his fingers digging into the mattress. He was too old for fairy tales. Tying Allie to him with marriage vows was one thing. Her sleeping with him was quite another.

Five years later every word Allie had thrown at
him the night he'd gone to tell her about the baby
still burned in his head. Zane had agonized over his
decision to marry Kim. No, that wasn't true. He'd
understood almost at once what he had to do.
Because of Zane's selfish, juvenile behavior, an innocent baby, his baby, was coming into the world.
He couldn't walk away from the consequences. The
baby was his responsibility.

The agony came from knowing he'd failed to protect Allie. As innocent as his unborn baby, she'd
suffered the repercussions of his abominable behavior.

What he'd done was unforgivable, but he'd hoped
that Allie, who'd grown up with an absentee father,
would know he couldn't allow his baby to be raised
without a father. Even if she didn't forgive him for
sleeping with Kim, he'd believed Allie would understand his decision.

Never in his worst nightmares had he dreamed
Allie would hate Hannah.

There it was. The thing he kept avoiding. The
thing he didn't want to think about. The words Allie
had said this evening. She'd apologized. Said she
no longer felt that way. Zane wanted to believe her.

How could she hate Hannah? Hannah was the
best thing in his life. If Allie had seen Hannah as
he had... A red, shriveled-up peanut who'd wailed
her way into his heart. A chubby baby kicking her
legs as he changed her diapers. Allie had missed
Hannah's first smiles, first steps, first words.

He was a fool. In nature, females bonded with their young through the miracle of birth. How could he expect Allie to fall instantly in love with another woman's child?

Persuading a reluctant Allie to marry him was crazy. A man couldn't rewrite the past, and he was the last man who deserved a happy ending. He didn't know if the Allie he loved existed anymore. Maybe he'd killed that Allie.

She still connected with animals like no one else. He'd watched her rubbing her mare. And craved her hands rubbing him.

She couldn't have changed that much. Hannah trusted her, and Hannah didn't give her trust lightly. Allie would be good to his daughter. He'd let Hannah work her magic. No one could be around Hannah for long and not fall in love with her.

Allie could be the mother Hannah had never had.

Zane yearned for her to be the wife he had never had.

Happiness insidiously crept through him. He was finally bringing Allie Lassiter to his home where she belonged.

He loved Allie. He needed her. The marriage would work out. It had to. He couldn't bear it if he had to give up Allie again.

Zane pressed his palms against the bottom sheet. Smooth and cool, before warming to his touch. Like Allie's breasts. His blood and a few other parts stirred.

He wanted Allie in his bed.

*   *   *

"Mom sent me up to tell you we're all ready down-stairs." Greeley stuck her head in the doorway.

"I'm not getting married."

Greeley looked from Cheyenne's wedding dress hanging on the closet door to the tumble of nylon stockings and white shoes on the floor beside Allie's childhood bed. "I'll tell Mom." The door closed silently behind her.

Allie plopped down on the bed and stared at her bedroom at the Double Nickel ranch as if she'd never seen it. As if she hadn't spent hundreds of nights drifting asleep in this bed to dream of Zane. Girlish dreams in a girlish room with a lavender chenille bedspread and dotted Swiss curtains fluttering in the early evening breeze. Lilacs sprigged the creamy wallpaper. Rectangles of less-faded paper disclosed where pictures had been removed. Pictures of Zane. Taken down and trashed.

Earlier Allie had watched Zane and Hannah drive under the old wooden arch at the main entrance to the ranch. Allie's great-great-grandmother had painted the faded sign tacked to the side of the gate. Hope Valley, Anna Nichols had called the area, as she and her new husband began both their marriage and their ranch here. Allie didn't share her ancestor's vision of a hopeful future.

Zane had used Hannah's needs to manipulate Allie, to rip apart every argument she'd mustered. Arguing half the night, he'd worn her down.

A scheduled tour on Sunday and making the necessary wedding arrangements today had kept her too busy to think. In a daze, she'd met Zane this morning to pick up a marriage licence.

Marriage license. Couldn't anyone see how preposterous this whole idea was? Zane's sister couldn't come but she'd phoned, bubbling with congratulations. Zane's parents had flown up from Texas. They were in the living room. Allie's mother had telegraphed Cheyenne and Thomas, still on their honeymoon in some exotic location.

Allie and Zane had not planned a honeymoon.

There had been no wedding rehearsal, no prenuptial dinner. Allie had refused to sully a church with a wedding that made a mockery of marriage.

She could not marry Zane Peters.

A soft knock preceded Mary Lassiter's entrance. "You were dressed for a wedding when I went downstairs thirty minutes ago. What changed your mind?"

"I'm not getting married, that's all." Allie rolled over on her stomach. She hadn't changed her mind. She'd come to her senses. "Tell everyone to go home."

"Including the groom?" her mother asked quietly.

"Especially the groom."

"When you called yesterday morning and said you and Zane had decided to get married, I wanted so badly for you to be happy, I didn't ask enough questions. Then I got caught up in the details of the wedding. You said you didn't want any fuss, but I couldn't let a daughter of mine get married without a wedding cake, even if it is just a cake from a mix." Her mother sat on the edge of the bed. "Your Grandpa Yancy used to accuse me of being blinded by romance, and I've done it again."

Allie buried her head in her pillow so her mother wouldn't see the moisture filling her eyes. Although why she felt like crying, Allie had no idea. Maybe bridal nerves, even if she had no intention of being a bride.

Her mother gently rubbed Allie's back. "Want to talk about it?"

Allie shook her head.

"May I come in?" Worth's voice came from the hallway. Not waiting for permission, he entered and closed the door behind him. "Greeley says you've changed your mind."

"I suppose you've come to tell me Dolly and Buck flew up from Texas, the judge is here and Mom's baked a cake, so it's too late to change my mind," Allie said into the pillow.

"Actually I want to know if I can go ahead and eat the cake since you're not getting married. Chocolate's my favorite."

"Worth!" his mother said half laughing, half protesting.

Allie raised her head indignantly to glare at her brother. The love and understanding she read on his face broke through her defenses, and she stared blurry-eyed at a wallpaper flower. "What did everyone say?" She wouldn't ask about Zane's reaction.

"Mom thought we ought to talk to you before making any grand announcement."

Allie saw the look of inquiry he directed at their mother. "I'm not changing my mind."

"Nobody's forcing you to get married," Worth said, sitting on the other side of the bed.

"Good, because I'm not."

Mary stood up. "I'll go down and tell everyone." She left a silent void in the bedroom.

"Go ahead." Allie finally said to her brother. "Get it off your chest. The big lecture. How I shouldn't expect Mom to do my dirty work. Now everyone is here."

"Don't worry about it. Dolly and Buck are making a fuss over Hannah. The judge has been buzzing around Mom. I think he'd like to be her best beau." Worth uttered a derisive laugh. "Bad choice of words. The last thing Mom needs is another Beau."

Allie turned her head. "He wasn't much of a father."

"Beau would have been the first to agree with you."

"A child needs two parents."

"We managed with one."

"We had Grandpa," Allie reminded him.

Worth studied her with somber eyes. "Is that what this sudden wedding is about? Giving Hannah a mother? I should have guessed. Before Cheyenne got married all she talked about was how much she loved Thomas. Neither you nor Zane mentioned love."

Allie shrugged. She didn't need Worth to tell her how dumb she'd almost been.

"Hannah's a little cutie, I'll give you that. All dressed up in a fluffy pink dress. She came equipped with color markers so everyone could sign her cast." He chuckled. "Davy's so jealous he doesn't have a broken arm, he can't see straight."

"What about..." Allie buried her face back in the pillow.

"Zane?" Worth must have taken the sound she made for "yes," because he continued, "He's all spiffed up. Guess he thought he was getting married."

"That's not funny." Allie lifted her head. "I haven't heard any cars leave."

"Mom probably told everyone to stay for dinner."

She gave him a startled look. "How could everyone just sit down and eat?"

"You know Mom. She's not going to send anyone away with an empty stomach because you're calling off the wedding."

"I can't go down and face Zane. Am I supposed to hide up here forever?"

"I don't know. Are you hiding?"

"I knew you couldn't pass up an opportunity for a sermon. Do your duty, Alberta. Remember who you are, Alberta. How is your behavior going to make your mother feel, Alberta? Do you think your mother is going to approve, Alberta? Does behaving that way make you feel good, Alberta?"

"I don't remember those words passing my lips just now."

"You were thinking them."

He patted her shoulder. "Marriage is a big step, Allie. We all want you to be happy, but you're the one who has to decide what's right for you."

"I have decided. I'm not getting married."

"Okay." The mattress rebounded as he stood. "If you can't face Zane, I'll bring you up some supper on a tray."

Allie rolled over and sat up. "I hate you, Fort Worth Beauregard Lassiter. You're being nice and offering to bring up food to make me feel guilty and like a coward for not facing everyone myself. You think I should have told Zane, don't you?"

"He's in the hall. Want me to tell him to come in?"

Giving her brother a killing look, Allie nodded, then grabbed her pillow and hugged it to her stomach. The pillow did nothing to fill the emptiness deep inside her.

Worth left the room. Male voices rumbled in the hall.

"You hear any of that?" Worth asked.

Zane nodded. "I should have dragged her to the courthouse first thing this morning." He would have, but his parents had insisted on coming for the wedding and hadn't been able to get a flight out of San Antonio until today. He loved his mother, but he'd wanted to tell her he didn't give a damn whether she made it to the wedding, as long as Allie made it. He should have told her. The extra time had given Allie too long to think.

"Allie thinks it's about Hannah, but it's not, not for you, is it?"

"What do you think?"

"I think you may have given yourself an impossible task. If there's one thing the Lassiter sisters have in common, it's that they have got to be the three stubbornest women on earth. Mom's tough and a fighter, but she's never been as pigheaded as her daughters. They got it from Yancy." Worth paused. "Whatever Allie decides, all the Lassiters will support her decision." He headed downstairs.

In the bedroom, Zane closed the door behind him. Allie wore her unreadable face, but her eyes gave her away. Wariness mixed with belligerence. He wanted to fling her over his shoulder and haul her downstairs. Stand her in front of the judge. Make her say the wedding vows. Damn it, he'd come so close.

"Hannah was excited about us getting married," he said. "She insisted on wearing her party dress."

"You can't make me feel guilty. Not when you came to me only weeks before our last attempt at a wedding and told me you'd slept with another woman and were going to marry her."

Zane pushed back his jacket and put his hands in his pockets. "Should I scream at you the way you screamed at me?"

"How was I supposed to react? Congratulate

you? Wish you all the happiness in the world? No woman could do that. I'd ordered flowers, a cake, my wedding dress, the invitations.''

"A point you made repeatedly that night. I'd screwed up our whole lives and all you could think about was how I'd screwed up your wedding plans.''

"You never gave me a choice. Everyone else had choices, but not me. You and Kim chose to sleep together. You chose to marry her. Nobody cared what I thought. Did you even think about marrying me and adopting Kim's baby? Did you ever once consider I might be willing to overlook what you'd done?''

"Would you have overlooked it?''

"No, but I should have had the choice,'' she said in a low voice, watching her hands knead the pillow in her lap.

"Why? Would turning me down have made you feel better?''

She raised her head and glared defiantly at him. "At least I would have had the satisfaction of telling you I wouldn't marry you if you were the last man on earth.''

"Is that what this is about?''

She shook her head. "It's about not making a stupid mistake. This time I have a choice, and I choose not to marry you.''

Zane walked over to the window and stared out. "I didn't have a choice,'' he said quietly. "Not about marrying Kim.'' Overhead a turkey vulture

wheeled in the sky. Allie's elderly mare stood in the
corral facing the house. He'd driven his pickup with
the horse trailer hitched on back so they could trailer
the mare back to his place. The setting sun bur-
nished Copper's coat to a fiery red.

"When Kim came to me and told me about the
baby, at first I thought I had choices." The horror
of the moment, the panic, the utter despair, revisited
Zane. He clutched the keys in his pocket. "I didn't
want to believe her. I wanted the whole situation to
go away. I wanted to turn back time. I thought, if
she went away, gave away the baby, if there was
no baby, you wouldn't need to know. I wanted to
offer her money, anything, to make it all go away.
She was crying, going on and on, and as she talked,
I realized, it was my baby she was talking about.
My baby. I wanted her to give away my baby. I
wanted to ignore my baby. For no other reason than
a baby was inconvenient."

Allie made no sound behind him.

Zane forced himself to continue. "I never
claimed to be perfect, but I had to face a hard truth
at that moment about just how imperfect I was. I
thought it was the lowest point in my life. It
wasn't."

His keys bit deep into his palm. "Much worse
was telling you. The look on your face... The disbelief, the pain, the contempt." Her look of shock
and abhorrence had replayed in his brain a million
times. "I deserved every bit of your contempt. I'd

behaved despicably.'' He exhaled deeply. "I can't tell you how sorry I am.''

Zane knew apologies changed nothing. He'd been a fool to think his past was a prison from which he could win parole. He'd danced. He had to pay the piper. He was too old to whine about the length of the dance.

Turning, he rested his hip on the windowsill. "The other night I persuaded you to marry me for Hannah's sake, and you agreed out of a sense of guilt.'' He noted her tiny start. Hadn't she realized he'd guessed that?

"We thought we could go through a ceremony,'' he said, "live in the same house, eat at the same table, and sleep in different beds. I was willing to take you on any terms, but the way we've been going, dwelling on past crimes, nursing hurts, trying to strike first... You're right, it wouldn't have worked. Hannah suffered through one unhappy marriage. I'm not going to put her through another.''

Allie sat on her bed, her knees drawn up beneath her chin. She didn't look at him. "That's nothing to me. I'm not marrying you.''

Zane knew he should let it go. Walk away. He couldn't. There had to be a way. When the idea came to him, he was too desperate to stop and analyze it for flaws.

He had nothing to lose.

Gripping his keys, he bet the rest of his life on the biggest gamble he'd ever taken. "I want us to get married, Allie. Hear me out,'' he said fiercely as she opened her mouth. "Marry me, give me one month of a real marriage. One month. If we can't work things out between us, we'll call it quits. I'll figure out a way to fight Vern and Edie."

In the distance a horse neighed. In the bedroom, silence reigned. Zane had a sense of time stopped as he waited for Allie's answer.

She stirred, then slowly faced him. "A real marriage? Why don't you come out and say it, Zane? You want to sleep with me."

He hadn't slept with another woman since he'd married Kim. The only woman he'd ever wanted to sleep with sat across the room. "I want to sleep with you."

Allie put her head down on her knees. "Go away."

Zane hesitated. There must be words he could use to sway her. Words to force her into marrying him. None came to him. His gamble had lost. He went downstairs to collect his daughter to take her home.

Allie threw her pillow across the room. Zane Peters had more nerve than anyone she knew. After what he'd done, he actually expected her to consider a real marriage?

If he'd wanted to marry her for real, he should have done it five years ago. He should have known she didn't mean it when she'd told him she'd never marry him, but no, he'd used their argument as an excuse to sleep with another woman.

What kind of glutton for punishment did he think

she was? She wasn't about to give him a chance to devastate her again. Not that he could. Not when she didn't care two hoots about him. Or about how wide his shoulders looked in his wedding suit. Or how handsome he looked.

How dare he ask her to forget the past? Which is exactly what his outrageous offer amounted to. Pretend he hadn't betrayed her? She had no intention of pretending anything.

Did he think a stupid apology wiped out the pain he'd inflicted on her? If he'd suffered one tiny fraction of what she'd suffered, he'd know it took more than words to even the score.

Anger pumping through her veins, Allie jumped up and paced the width of the bedroom. For his sins, Zane had been rewarded with a daughter he idolized. Allie had done nothing but love him and she'd been jilted. Been pitied by the entire population up and down the Roaring Fork River. She'd suffered through five barren, empty years. He'd ripped up her heart, ruined her life, even stolen the name of her first daughter. In return he expected her to live with him as husband and wife in every sense.

As if she'd been waiting for him for five years. Pining away for him.

She didn't want to marry him. She wanted to bang his head against a stone wall. She wanted to drive a herd of cattle over him and pound him into the dirt. She wanted to hurt him.

She wanted revenge.

Allie stopped dead in the middle of her room.

She wanted revenge. Only by Zane suffering the way she'd suffered could the slate be wiped clean.

She'd be done with Zane Peters once and for all. She didn't want marriage. She wanted revenge.

Cheyenne's wedding dress caught her eye, and the perfect plan popped into Allie's head. Marriage and revenge could be one and the same.

One month, Zane had said. Allie would give him a real marriage for one month. She'd be the perfect wife, weaving herself so thoroughly into his life, he couldn't imagine living without her. She'd occupy his days, his mind, his bed.

The thought of his bed brought her up short. How could she sleep with a man she didn't love? Allie mentally slapped herself. People did it all the time. Zane had slept with a woman he claimed he didn't love. Allie was an adult. Twenty-six years old. She could make love to him.

It wouldn't be making love. Having sex. A purely physical activity, which had nothing to do with love. Like washing her face or brushing her teeth. One merely went through the drill. Get from point A to point B. He'd never know her emotions weren't engaged. She could fake it.

Sharing a bed with Zane shouldn't be too difficult. Even without love, lingering remnants of the attraction she'd once felt for him occasionally resurfaced. The remains of a purely physical, meaningless attraction.

Hannah. What about Hannah? Hannah would see Allie as someone visiting for a month. They could have fun together and then Allie would leave. The way Zane's parents visited the ranch and then returned to Texas. It wasn't as if Allie planned to be Hannah's mother. Hannah had her father. And Ruth. Once Allie left, Hannah would forget her as if Allie had never been there.

Allie contemplated Cheyenne's bridal veil carefully spread out on the surface of her bureau. She could raise a million objections. Or she could just do it.

She would do it.

She'd make Zane Peters fall in love with her. She'd bring him to his knees.

Then she'd walk out on him.

As he'd walked out on her.

Whoever'd said revenge was sweet had never made it clear exactly how sweet it could be. Allie smiled. If she were Amber, she'd purr.

Downstairs a chair scraped against the floor. People must be starting to leave. Zane would be leaving. And the judge. Snatching the bridal veil from the top of the bureau, Allie plopped it on her head.

She stopped at the bottom of the staircase to look into the dining room. Everyone sat around the table except Worth, who stood with a large knife in his hand. The wedding cake sat in front of him.

"The bride and groom are supposed to cut the cake," Allie said loudly. "After the wedding."

All conversation instantly ceased.

Mary Lassiter spoke first. "Allie? What is going

on? Blue jeans and a bridal veil? What are you doing?''

''Allie!'' Hannah waved a fork.

''I thought you weren't getting married,'' Davy said.

Watching Zane, Allie ignored the others. He sat with his back to her. His body had jerked when she'd spoken, then every single muscle in his back had rigidly locked. Allie waited.

Finally Zane turned, his face composed. One eyebrow rose quizzically. ''We can wait until you're dressed.''

''We can wait longer than that,'' Mary said. ''Allie, I want to see you in the kitchen.'' Once there, Mary closed the door to the dining room. ''What's going on? A few minutes ago you were determined not to marry Zane.''

Allie shrugged. ''Call it bridal nerves.''

Zane walked into the kitchen. ''I think I ought to be part of this discussion.''

Mary Lassiter looked at him. ''I don't know what you said to her, but I know you want her to be sure she's doing the right thing.''

''I am doing the right thing.''

''I ought to lock you in your room.''

''You can't stop me, Mom. If you're opposed, I'll get married somewhere else, but I've made up my mind.'' Allie looked directly at Zane. ''I'm marrying Zane. Now.''

Zane stared calmly back at her. The kitchen smelled of cake and baked chicken.

After a moment, her mother said, "You can't wear blue jeans. If you don't want to wear Cheyenne's bridal gown, at least put on a dress."

Allie rammed one last pin into the veil's simple headpiece. Her gaze never left Zane's face. "Take it or leave it."

"I'll take it." The simple words resonated with layers of meaning.

Her heart rate tripled at the look in his eyes. A look quickly extinguished. She refused to acknowledge the second thoughts clamoring insistently in her head.

Zane held out his hand. "I'm ready when you are."

Her courage—or foolhardiness?—threatened to flee. She'd never be ready. Zane wrapped his strong, work-callused hand around her hand. A heated current flowed from him to her. She'd forgotten how dark blue his irises were. Dark blue with white flecks. Amusement and approval warmed his eyes. No, she wanted to shout. Don't approve. "I'm not doing this for you," she muttered.

"I know."

He thought she was doing it for Hannah. She couldn't go through with it. Allie tried to pull her hand free, but Zane tightened his grip, lifting her hand to his lips. Electricity zapped through her body. No. He couldn't make love to her. Not here. Not now.

"Alberta Harmony Lassiter, will you marry me?"

She tried to shake her head, to refuse, but her chin had a mind of its own and somehow lifted up and down. Zane scrutinized her face. He must read the panic in her eyes. He'd release her. Banish the spell.

A crooked smile curved his mouth. "Let's go tell the judge we're ready," he said, his eyes intent on Allie's face.

"Allie." Worth came into the kitchen, followed by Greeley. "Wait until you're sure what you're doing."

"I'm sure." She knew her voice lacked conviction.

Zane gave her hand a quick squeeze. "Quit acting like a big brother, Worth. Allie knows what she's doing."

He knew. He'd guessed she wanted revenge. Allie dismissed the thought as soon as it entered her mind. Zane couldn't possibly know. Not yet. In one month. When she left him. She had no misgivings, no doubts. This is what she wanted to do. Definitely. Dividing a glittering smile between her brother and her bridegroom, she said, "Let's get this show on the road."

"Allie," Worth began.

Greeley cut him off. "Unless you plan to tie her to her bed and lock her bedroom door, you know you're not going to stop her once she's made up her mind."

"I want to be sure she's the one who made up her mind. I don't want her pressured into anything."

"She's not ten," Greeley said. "She's an adult.

She can make her own decisions. She knows the child needs a mom.''

"That's no reason to allow Zane to talk her into something against her better judgment," Worth retorted. "Marriage is a serious commitment. Allie wants a husband she can trust to stick by her. I'm not sure she sees Zane as that husband."

"You can't expect her to ignore the child's needs," Greeley said.

"Worth. Greeley. I know you're concerned, but this is Allie's decision to make," Mary said quietly. "Don't bring your own prejudices into it."

An awkward silence hung in the kitchen. Allie's gaze went from Greeley's and Worth's embarrassed faces to her mother's moist eyes. "In case everyone's forgotten," Allie said loudly, "I'd like to get married, and I'd like to do it before the twenty-fifth century." She walked out of the kitchen with Zane.

Her mother followed them into the dining room and gave Allie a wry, loving smile. "But not in blue jeans."

Zane grinned at Mary. "It's okay, Mary. We'll have something to laugh about on our fiftieth wedding anniversary."

Allie managed to laugh with everyone else in spite of the sinking feeling deep in her midsection. The smell of food had affected her empty stomach. "Let's get married so I can eat."

"Wait!" Hannah scrambled down from her perch of phone books stacked on a chair and darted from the dining room. She returned clutching a bunch of bedraggled wildflowers. "Flowers," she said triumphantly. "I picked 'em. For throwing."

"Oh, Hannah," Mary said in dismay, "I forgot about your flowers. I should have put them in water. I'm sorry."

Allie took the half-dead flowers. "They're perfect." Everyone smiled approvingly. They thought she was being polite. She wasn't. Half-dead flowers suited a marriage that was an ending, not a beginning.

Standing in front of the fireplace beside Zane, Allie said firmly to the judge, "Keep it simple. Leave out all that for better and worse and obeying stuff. I take him and he takes me and you pronounce us married. That's it."

Married.

The two of them alone. Hannah was spending the night with his parents and the Lassiters at the Double Nickel ranch.

Zane set Allie's suitcases on the porch. He'd never really believed Allie would marry him.

He knew she'd expected him to argue about omitting the obeying bit in the wedding vows. Wouldn't matter if she did promise to obey. Allie would do whatever the hell she wanted. He wouldn't have her any other way. And he had her.

For at least one month he had her.

He opened his front door.

Whatever her reasons for going through with the wedding.

She might fool Worth and Greeley into thinking she'd married him for Hannah's sake, but Zane knew darned well Allie's reasons had nothing to do with his daughter.

He suspected she'd married him to make his life a living hell. She gave herself too much credit. It wasn't in Allie to treat others badly. A guilty conscience inevitably got in her way.

Turning, he swept her up into his arms.

"What are you doing? Put me down."

He carried her into the house. "Welcome home, Mrs. Peters." He liked the sound of it. Myriad expressions crossed Allie's face. Most too fleeting for him to decipher. He wanted her to throw her arms around him and kiss him.

She fixed a smile on her face and stared at his left ear. "Thank you."

Zane stood her back on her feet. "I'll take your bags up." Allie's footsteps echoed his as she followed him.

To the bedrooms. Tension hummed through him. And need. By marrying him, Allie had agreed to a real marriage, even if she'd never said it in so many words. Zane stopped in the hallway. She'd said he hadn't given her a choice before. He took a deep breath. He didn't want to, but he'd give her a choice tonight.

"Hannah sleeps in what was the guest bedroom, and I've been sleeping in my old room." Belatedly he realized that, between the wedding, caring for Hannah with her broken arm and the haying, he'd neglected to consider the master bedroom. Noisily he cleared his throat. ''It's been a long day. If you'd prefer, that is, since Hannah's not here, if you want to sleep in her room tonight...''

''Why not in...'' Allie's voice died as she opened the door to the master bedroom. ''Did your mom change her mind about leaving her furniture and take it to Texas with her?''

''It's in the attic.'' Kim had replaced pieces that had been in his family for years with cheap laminated blond furniture.

''I always loved your folks' bedroom,'' Allie said faintly.

''The flowered wallpaper had faded, and Kim didn't like dark walnut furniture.'' The psychedelic wallpaper in black and silver with red fuzzy stuff and the shiny pink, frilly curtains literally turned his stomach.

''What happened to your great-grandmother's quilt?''

''I put it away until Hannah gets older.''

Allie tentatively poked the bed, jerking her hand back when the bed moved. ''It's a water bed. With a fuchsia satin spread.'' She bit her lower lip and avoided looking at him. ''There's purple shag carpet over the hardwood floor.''

That couldn't be awe he heard in her voice. ''After Kim died, I closed the door to this room,'' he said stiffly. ''No one comes in here except Ruth to dust.''

Allie cautiously sat on the bed, gingerly bounced

the water bed mattress, then threw herself backward with her arms outstretched. Looking up, her eyes widened. "I can't decide if it's like an old-fashioned bordello or one of those honeymoon places which advertise in bridal magazines."

Kim would be happy to know her bordello theme had been immediately recognized. Zane looked up to see Allie's face reflected in the mirrored tiles fixed to the ceiling. "You don't have to sleep in here," he said curtly.

The tiles mirrored Allie's sheepish smile. "I'm sorry. That was tacky." Her smile turned to a frown. "I'm not sure I can sleep in here. I think they'd give me nightmares. Like a hundred me staring at me. Aren't they a little dangerous? What if one fell? If it didn't cut a person to pieces, it'd slice up the water bed and we'd drown."

She'd said "we." Zane forgot the surroundings as hope lurched within him.

"On the other hand," she continued before he could speak, "when you think about it, it seems a shame to waste what most newly-wedded couples pay big bucks for." In the mirror her gaze skittered past his reflection, and she seemed to be studying a far corner of the ceiling. "Maybe we ought to investigate the possibilities. For Thomas. He could install mirrored ceilings in his hotels. They're supposed to be sexy." She picked at a button on her shirt. "Do you want to sleep in here?"

His and Kim's marriage had been a disaster from the start. Wounded by his inability to love her, Kim had retaliated the only way she knew how. Zane had given her his loyalty while she lived. He refused to condemn her in death. The bedroom, a harsh symbol of how he'd failed Kim, sickened and saddened Zane.

Ruth had thoroughly cleaned and aired the room so Zane knew the scent of cheap perfume hanging in the air existed only in his imagination. He had no idea how many men Kim had entertained on this bed. He'd never been one of them. ''I'm not sleeping in here with you,'' he said to Allie. Turning on his heel, he left the room.

CHAPTER FIVE

ALLIE stared after him in total disbelief. Before the
wedding, Zane had said he wanted to sleep with her.
She'd married him, resolved to sleep with him—
admittedly for reasons of her own—and he was rejecting her? She fought her way off the undulating
bed and marched into the hall.

Zane's bedroom door stood open and she charged
into his room. He stopped in the middle of removing
his suit coat. "What's that supposed to mean?" she
demanded. "You talked me into this stupid marriage and you're refusing to sleep with me? You
can't refuse." Dragging her gaze from his broad,
white-shirted chest, Allie doggedly continued with
her grievance. "I'm the only one in this marriage
who's allowed to refuse to sleep with anyone." An
explanation for his behavior suddenly occurred to
her. "I'm too skinny, aren't I? I'm well aware your
wife was built like a centerfold model, but—"

"You're not skinny." Zane shrugged out of his
coat and tossed it across the back of a chair.
"You're just right." Unbuttoning his shirt came
next. He unbuttoned maddeningly slow.

Allie wanted to rip his shirt open. "Then why don't you want to sleep with me?"

His shirt went the way of his coat. "Who said I didn't?" Sitting on the edge of the bed, Zane tugged off his boots.

"You did. You said you weren't sleeping with me."

"In there." Zane stood and walked purposefully around the bed. "I didn't say anything about sleeping with you in here."

The look in his eyes propelled her backward. "This is an awfully small bed, and I'm a restless sleeper. I kick off the covers and stuff." She backed into a wall. "You won't be able to get any sleep."

Zane braced his hands against the wall on either side of her head. "Sleeping's the last thing on my mind tonight."

She couldn't look away from him. The raw need and desire burning in his eyes took her breath away. For a second she panicked, and raised her hands to his chest to push him away. His body heat warmed her palms. Impossible not to slide her hands over his smooth, tight skin. He didn't move. Unless one counted his quickened breathing or the slight tensing of his muscles. Tiny hard bumps pressed against her fingers. Bumps Allie wanted to explore.

Zane's eyes darkened. "You said you're the only one who gets to refuse to sleep with anyone. Are you refusing?"

"What if I am?" Her thumb caught on his nipple. A small, ragged sound came from him. "Your choice. I told you," he said in a husky voice. "I won't kiss you again until you want me to."

"Oh, that." Allie trailed a finger along the edge of his collarbone. "I thought agreeing to marry you took care of that business." She risked looking up at him.

A tiny smile played at one corner of his mouth. "Does that mean you want me to kiss you?"

"Since when have you had to have all your t's crossed and your i's dotted?"

"I'll take that as yes." Moving his hands to cup her breasts, Zane lowered his head.

Allie closed her eyes at the first touch of his lips against hers. Nothing about their deal said he had to nibble her bottom lip or outline her mouth with his tongue or deepen the kiss until her entire insides turned to flame and nothing existed except for his kiss.

And his hands. His hands couldn't be ignored as they caressed her breasts through her clothing, and then through the wisp of lingerie she wore. When nothing separated her breasts from his work-toughened hands, she knew exactly how dangerous Zane Peters could be.

His ever-deepening attention to her mouth turned pleasure into need. With a quiet moan, Allie dropped back her head, giving him fuller access, surrendering, and at the same time demanding. The outside world faded. Nothing existed but Zane's mouth and the magic he worked on hers. When he finally abandoned her mouth to trail tiny kisses along the side of her face and around the outer edges of her ear, she was clinging to him for support.

And stark naked.

"You're going to freeze." Zane picked her up and carried her to his bed.

The bedsheets were icy cold. Then Zane joined her, his long, lean body warming her from their touching lips to the tips of her toes. Their lower bodies tangled, and the hairs on his legs rasped erotically against her sensitized skin. Allie slid her hands over his shoulders, taking pleasure in the width, the warmth, the strength of them.

Zane lifted his head, his face inches from hers. "I've pictured your head on my pillow so many times..." He brushed a kiss against her lips. "You have the sexiest mouth in creation."

"It's the same mouth Cheyenne has."

He shook his head. "It's sexier on you."

Muddled, needy sensations built up deep within her, and she moved restlessly beneath him.

"Oh, Allie," he said with a half laugh, half gasp. And then his mouth devoured her.

She'd never dreamed it would be like this. Just body parts slipping and sliding and coming together, but somehow... Hands and fingers and mouths and lips and tongues... Secret places and age-old movements. Spiraling need and exhilaration and a slow circling back to earth. Two hearts pounding in unison.

She didn't need to fake it.

Zane lifted his weight from her and pulled the covers up to her chin. He lay beside her, his side barely touching hers. "Thank you. That was nice."

Nice. All warm, fuzzy feelings toward him evaporated. Nice. Allie hated nice.

Everyone had praised her for being nice about Zane marrying another woman. Called her nice because she refused to say a word against him or the woman he'd married. They'd endlessly hashed and rehashed the details of her niceness.

Nice was for well-bred older ladies who served you tea. Nice was for polite little girls on the Hyman Avenue Mall who asked permission to pet your dog. Nice was for courteous teenagers who held doors for you when your arms were full of packages.

What happened in Zane's bed had nothing to do with nice.

Allie would bet Zane had never called sex with Kim nice.

If he'd told Allie he loved her after they'd had sex, she might have tried to convince herself he wasn't lying. She might have considered abandoning thoughts of revenge.

Instead he'd called making love to her—no, having sex with her—nice. If she'd been at all ambivalent about seeking revenge—which she hadn't—Allie no longer was. Zane Peters had given her an engraved invitation to do her worst.

She'd show him nice.

*   *   *

His eyes closed, Zane lay on his back, savoring the heat from Allie's bottom tucked up against his side.

She'd said nothing about love. He didn't deserve the words, but the omission ate at him. After they'd made love, Allie had rolled over and gone to sleep. When he'd awakened her during the night, she'd willingly, but wordlessly, made love with him.

He knew better than to speak words of love to her.

With every kiss, every touch, he'd tried to show her how much he loved her. He'd relished the tiny sounds she'd made in the back of her throat, the way her body had tightened and vibrated before collapsing against him.

Loving each other for the first time, there'd been awkward moments, none of which detracted from the sheer joy and satisfaction of finally having Allie in his bed. The night had surpassed anything he'd experienced. Surpassed his dreams.

In the beginning he'd tried to be an adequate lover for Kim. Sadly she'd guessed he had to try. Her reactions had ranged from seduction to pleading to rage. She'd begged him to tell her she was as good in bed as Allie. Kim had never believed he and Allie hadn't made love.

They'd made love last night.

They'd make love again tonight.

He'd laid his proposal before Allie. One month as his wife. By marrying him, she'd agreed, even if she'd never said the words. One month to win, not her forgiveness, but a second chance. One month to prove to her he wasn't the irresponsible person he'd been five years ago. One month to convince her she belonged with him.

Unable to stop himself, Zane ran his hand along Allie's bare hip. Reassuring himself. Her leg slid the length of his.

"Good morning, Mrs. Peters."

"Ms. Lassiter," she said sleepily.

"Don't tell me I married a liberated woman."

She rolled over to face him. Under the covers her fingers playfully investigated his belly button, then glided downward. "Is that a problem?"

"I don't know. I'm an old-fashioned kind of guy." Zane dug his fingers into the mattress to keep from tossing her on her back. "As a former teacher, maybe you could educate me on the advantages of having a liberated woman for a wife."

"I'd be happy to."

She was one hell of a teacher.

Leaning back against the passenger seat, Zane tugged his wide-brimmed hat down over his face. "I could get used to being married to a liberated woman."

"Don't." Allie hoped he didn't notice the heat crawling up her face. Her campaign to become the woman Zane couldn't live without before she dumped him didn't require the level of enthusiasm she'd shown this morning. "It was a one-time aberration."

"I'm talking about you doing the driving. I have a feeling you're referring to something else."

She decided to ignore the amusement in his voice. "It makes more sense to take my car since I have to swing by the condo and pick up a few things. Worth is leaving Moonie there before he meets us for dinner at St. Chris's. The back seat of your pickup would be too crowded with Hannah, Moonie and Amber's cage."

"Who's Amber?"

"My cat."

"That'll please Hannah. We have barn cats, but she's never had a cat in the house. She's thrilled to have you and Moonie moving in." He chuckled. "Maybe Moonie more than you. We have a couple of border collies on the ranch, but they hang around with Wally at his and Ruth's place. I've tried to tell Hannah that Moonie is your dog, not hers, but I'm not sure she understands the distinction."

"Moonie's good with kids. Very patient. I used to take him to school on occasion. The kids loved him."

"Are you going to miss teaching?"

"I'll miss the kids. I won't miss grading papers or parent conferences. And leading tours is great for a couple of ex-teachers. A captive audience for our lectures."

"Did you cancel your tours for this week?"

"Had none. Now that school has started, things slow down until ski season. The aspen trees turning gold brings people on the weekends, but we seldom have anyone booked during the week.''

"Doesn't it depress you to haul around old people or disabled people?''

"Our clients might have special needs, but their courage and their refusal to allow themselves to be limited is inspirational. Dealing with small groups, we get to know our clients. Many are repeat customers who become almost like extended family.''

"I never heard how you got started.''

"Cheyenne backed into it. A friend asked for help with elderly grandparents, and that was such a success, word spread, and pretty soon Cheyenne decided there was a need for specialized tours for special people and special needs. She quit teaching and talked me into starting C and A Enterprises with her.

"We don't deal solely with physically challenged people. Sometimes it's elderly tourists who want to get out and do things, but at a slower pace, or parents who want trips geared to their children's needs. Basically we do small, personalized tours for family groups. It's fun to share the history and the wildlife of the area with tourists. Before Cheyenne's marriage I only worked during school holidays. We haven't figured out our new division of labor.''

"I've heard you take clients to the Double Nickel.''

"For the Western experience. Worth charms them and Mom feeds them.''

"You're welcome to bring them to my place.''

Ranch-type tours normally took place during the summer. By next summer there would be no question of Allie carting clients to Zane's ranch. She'd have left him long before that.

Pulling up in front of the St. Christopher Hotel, Allie said, "Right on time, and there's the welcoming party." Hannah, who stood with Buck Peters, enthusiastically waved.

Allie waved back, then handed her car keys to the bellman. Walking around her SUV, she joined the group on the sidewalk. From her perch in her father's arms, Hannah leaned toward Allie, her mouth puckered. Allie laughed and delivered the expected kiss. Hannah practically leaped from Zane's arms to Allie's.

Zane frowned. "She's too heavy for you."

"She's fine." Allie smiled at Zane's father who gave her a hearty hug and kiss. "Did you have a good time last night?"

"Me and Davy played. Davy's mommy is playing with angels like my mommy. So is his daddy. Davy has a new mommy. I didn't know kids can get new mommies."

Hannah chattered nonstop as Allie carried her through the three-story atrium lobby. The last rays of the sinking sun reached through the stained-glass ceiling to set the little girl's red hair aglow.

Allie stopped short inside the entrance to The Gilded Lily, St. Chris's ultraelegant dining room. She'd expected to see Zane's parents, her mom,

Worth, Greeley and Davy. She hadn't expected to see Cheyenne and Thomas.

"What are you two doing here?"

Thomas stood and kissed Allie's cheek. "Knowing your sister, you have to ask?" Extending his hand to Zane, he said, "Thomas Steele. It appears we're brothers-in-law."

Allie looked past them to her older sister. "Let me guess. You thought if you stayed away the whole two weeks of your honeymoon, I'd mess up things at the tour agency so badly, we'd have to declare bankruptcy."

"Don't be silly," Cheyenne said, her color high as she embraced her sister. "I wanted to congratulate the bride and groom." She edged Allie away from the others.

Allie raised an eyebrow. "Congratulate? Or interrogate? Worried about what you started when you invited Zane to your wedding?"

Cheyenne slid a glance over the child hanging around Allie's neck. "I won't be if you tell me how much in love you are."

"A little worry is good for the soul, isn't it?"

Cheyenne drew in a sharp breath. "I knew it. I told Thomas there was something wrong about this hasty business. Allie, what have you done? We tried to get back before the wedding, but we couldn't make it."

"You couldn't have stopped me."

"Stopped you from what?" Zane asked, reaching for his daughter. "Allie's held you long enough,

honey. You're a big girl. You can get down.'' He
set Hannah on the floor and she trotted off. Zane
looked at Allie, waiting for her answer.

Cheyenne hooked her arm in his. "From wearing
blue jeans to her wedding. Honestly, Zane, how
could you let her?"

He grinned. "Honestly, Cheyenne, for all I cared,
she could have worn a horse blanket.''

Greeley sat on one side of him, Cheyenne sat on
the other. They'd taken turns subtly pumping him
about his feelings for Allie. From time to time
they'd slipped in little comments that could be taken
as threats to his well-being if he treated their sister
badly again. Zane didn't mind playing their game.
Not as long as Allie sat across the table where he
could look at her.

He liked looking at his wife. Liked calling her
his wife.

Which was apparently more than Cheyenne did.
She'd lied about what she and Allie were talking
about. They'd been discussing Allie's marriage to
him. Allie had sounded very positive that Cheyenne
couldn't have stopped her.

Contentment settled over him. Once Allie had decided to go through with the wedding, she'd never
looked back. He certainly had no complaints about
his wedding night. His body tightened pleasantly.
He looked forward to repeating the experience. How
soon could they leave?

She looked beautiful, laughing with her brother

and Thomas Steele. If Zane hadn't seen the way Steele looked at Cheyenne, Zane might be tempted to punch his new brother-in-law in the nose.

Hannah sat sleepily on Allie's lap. His daughter had glued herself to Allie, and Allie had waved off his repeated offers to take Hannah. Listening to Worth, Allie absently smoothed down Hannah's unruly curls and lightly kissed the top of her head. Hannah turned up her face to beam a smile at Allie. Zane's throat constricted. His daughter and his wife. Allie wouldn't leave him after a month. They were a family now.

Hannah's head rested against Allie's breasts. They fit perfectly into his hands. He'd like to wrap his hands around them right now. He remembered the feel of them. As silky smooth as the light purple dress Allie wore. He'd touched her back to guide her into the restaurant. She hadn't needed guiding, but he liked touching her. The dress shimmered in the light and stretched across her breasts as Allie shifted.

He wanted to go home. To bed.

Allie's gaze met his and bright pink edged her cheeks. He had a feeling she knew exactly what he was thinking. She glanced over his shoulder and her face turned wary.

Vern Taylor's voice boomed out before Zane could turn. "Ruthie said you were here." Vern acknowledged Zane's parents, then said to Zane, "I got somebody in Belly's for you to meet."

Zane considered refusing, but knew his ex-in-laws would think nothing of creating a scene in one of Aspen's most exclusive hotels. Excusing himself, he left the table and followed Taylor into the bar room named over a hundred years ago for "Belly" Smith, an early miner in the area.

Edie Taylor sat on a stool at the Art Nouveau bar imported from France. Her ugly green pants outfit clashed with the saloon's red-and-white wallpaper. Occupied with patting her dyed black hair and primping in front of the huge mirror behind the carved bar, Edie didn't see Zane until he walked up behind her.

She flashed him a look of malicious triumph when he greeted her. "I want you to meet someone." Edie's red-painted mouth curved in a caricature of a smile. "This is Sean Doyle."

The unexpected blow slammed into Zane with the force of a gigantic wrecking ball. There could only be one reason for Edie and Vern to be with Doyle. They knew. Recognizing the calamitous consequences of their knowledge, Zane forced all expression from his face and held out his hand. "Doyle. I'm Zane Peters." Damn Vern and Edie. Damn Kim. He hadn't believed her. Hadn't wanted to believe her.

Doyle briefly shook Zane's hand, and muttered something. His gaze slid past Zane to dart around the room. The other patrons of Belly's pretended they didn't recognize the TV star.

Edie watched Zane with gloating eyes. "You

know who Sean is, don't you?'' Edie asked archly. She'd guessed he knew.

Zane had seen the situation comedy only once, but he had no trouble recognizing the man who starred in it. Not with that curly red hair. ''I've seen him on television.''

''Sean was a friend of Kim's. A very good friend.'' Edie drank a long swallow of her beer, dragging out the moment. ''He's Hannah's father.''

Zane thought he'd prepared himself. Now he realized nothing could prepare a man for having his worst nightmare brought to life. Unthinkable fears gripped him, and he clenched his fists, fighting for control. ''That's a hell of a sick joke, Edie. We both know I'm Hannah's father.'' He barely recognized the strained voice as his own.

''Do we?'' Edie asked in a nasty voice. ''Tell him what you told us, Sean.''

''It's true, Peters. Kimmie's kid is mine, and I want her.''

''Hannah is my daughter,'' Zane said, breathing heavily. ''I don't know what you hoped to accomplish by coming here with such an obscene lie, Doyle, but if you spread that damned lie around, I'm going to sue you for slander or libel or whatever the hell it is. It won't do your career much good. As for you—'' Zane glared at Edie and Vern ''—what kind of lousy parents are you? Telling lies and blackening your daughter's name. You ought to think about what's best for your granddaughter.''

"Kim's dead. Nothing can hurt her now," Vern said.

"What's best for a kid," Edie added, "is having her real father."

"I'm her real father," Zane said through gritted teeth.

"Don't be so all-fired sure of yourself," Edie said smugly.

Zane looked at his former mother-in-law. "What do you want?"

"I want what's right for Hannah." The sly triumph in her eyes made a mockery of her virtuous claim.

"How much money do you want?"

Edie assumed an air of injured innocence. "You can't buy my baby. The court will take the kid from you and give her to her rightful father."

"We're not fighting over Hannah in court and we're not dragging her mother's name through the mud. Hannah is mine." Zane turned to the actor who'd sat silently through Edie's and Zane's battle of words. "Damn it, Doyle. You can't do this to a child. It's inhuman. If you had any feeling at all for Kim, you'd forget this whole thing."

The man drew wet circles on the bar. "When she was pregnant, Kimmie told me the kid was mine. Said she wanted me to raise it."

Rage choked Zane, rendering him incapable of speech. He fought the anger. He couldn't give in to it. Not now. "Hannah's four. If Kim told you

Hannah was your child, why wait until now to speak up? Because it's a lie, that's why.''

The actor met Zane's gaze in the mirror, then dropped his eyes to the drink in front of him. ''I was married. Have a couple of boys. When Kimmie told me she was pregnant... I knew my wife would make a big stink. Divorce me. In the process, gouging me for every penny she could, and causing a big scandal.'' He picked up his drink, adding glumly. ''She's doing it anyway. Took the kids. Just because of some floozy out in California.'' He took a drink of beer. ''I can't help it if women throw themselves at me. It's not like I'm out looking for them.''

Another time the actor's aggrieved tone of voice might have amused Zane. Not now. ''I don't give a damn about your marital troubles, Doyle. Hannah is not your daughter. She's mine. You're not taking her away from me.''

''Sorry, Peters. I know how you feel, but the kid is mine. To tell the truth, I kind of forgot about her, but when I ran into Kimmie's folks at the bar where Kimmie used to work and told them I was sorry to hear about Kimmie, well, one thing led to another, and I told them about the kid being mine. They're right. I owe it to Kimmie to own up to my responsibility.'' He glanced at Zane's angry face and gulped a large swallow of beer. ''I mean, she is my kid. I'm just doing what's right.''

''Right for whom? An innocent child? A woman who's dead and can't defend her name? Or for a couple of mercenary people who see you as their gravy train?''

"Right for the kid. And for Kimmie," Doyle said.

"The hell you are." Talking to these three was a waste of time. Zane pivoted on his heel and turned to stone. Allie stood two feet away, a look of horror frozen on her face. "What do you want?" he snarled.

She looked from Zane to the Taylors and Doyle before her gaze returned to him. "Hannah's tired. I came to see if you're ready to leave."

"I'm ready to get the hell out of here," he said savagely and followed Allie back to The Gilded Lily where his daughter waited.

Sitting in the darkened living room, Allie watched Zane walk down the hall. The front door quietly opened and closed. The sound of footsteps stayed on the front porch. Pacing back and forth the length of the wooden porch.

He hadn't said a word to her as he'd followed her from Belly's back to the dining room. In the Gilded Lily, Zane had skillfully played the part of a man with nothing on his mind but saying goodbye to his relatives and taking his daughter home.

He'd said nothing during the quick stop at Allie's condo beyond asking for directions as he carried Allie's things to the car. Allie couldn't ask questions in front of Hannah.

The little girl fell asleep within minutes of leaving the lights of Aspen. Zane had slumped down in his seat and pulled his hat over his eyes. Discouraging conversation of any kind. Allie eventually turned the radio on low for company.

Back at his house, Zane talked and laughed with Hannah as they went through their nighttime rituals. Outwardly everything appeared normal. If Allie hadn't walked into Belly's when she did, she never would have suspected there was a thing wrong in Zane's world.

He would have shut her out. The way he was trying to shut her out now.

Not that she wanted to get involved. She'd heard enough to guess Sean Doyle had claimed he was Hannah's father. Why the television actor would say something so ludicrous defied comprehension.

Poor Hannah. Losing a mother hurt a child in so many ways, even if, as Allie suspected, Kim hadn't been much of a mother. How could she be with parents like hers? Beau hadn't been much of a father, but Mary Lassiter, with her father's help, had given her children the best home life she could.

Hannah had suffered more than enough. Marrying Zane for revenge didn't mean Allie couldn't help his daughter. And if helping Hannah meant interfering in Zane's business, then Allie would interfere. She half smiled. Cheyenne's meddling must be contagious.

Moonie came down the hall, restless in a house strange to him. Allie doubted he needed to go out again, but putting him out gave her an excuse to join Zane.

The mountains loomed dark against the night sky. Zane stood at the edge of the porch, his hands braced on the wooden railing, his head bowed. Moonie descended the porch steps and ambled across the yard toward a clump of high grass. Allie walked to Zane's side. "I brought out your jacket. These September nights are starting to get a little chilly." When he didn't reply, she draped his blue denim jacket over his shoulders.

After a minute, he shoved his arms into the sleeves. "Go to bed, Allie."

His bleak voice jolted her. And started a new train of thought. Until tonight, had Zane been ignorant of the fact, even though the rest of the valley knew, that his wife had played musical beds? The one betrayed was always the last to know. Satisfaction flowed over her. Let Zane see how he liked hearing that someone he trusted had slept with another person.

Rumor had Kim Taylor sleeping with any number of men. Zane and Sean Doyle ought to be commiserating with each other, not at each other's throats. The more Allie thought about it, the odder it seemed that the actor should claim to be Hannah's father. "I don't understand why Sean Doyle said he's Hannah's father."

"Did you see his hair?"

The abrupt question gave her pause. "Yes, but I—"

"Red and curly. Like Hannah's."

Allie frowned. Zane couldn't possibly be taking the actor's claim seriously. "Lots of people have red hair. Kim had red, curly hair. Not the exact same shade as Hannah's, but that's not unusual."

"Kim had light brown hair, straight as a string. The color and the curls came from the beauty shop."

"So there's red hair somewhere else in her family. Or in yours. Who knows why red hair pops out now and again? A lot of people have blond hair, but I don't think any of them could be a long, lost father of mine."

"Damn Kim." He beat his fist on the porch railing. "What did I ever do to her that she'd trick me that way? When she was pregnant I married her. I never questioned Hannah's paternity. I never believed—" His cut-off sentence hovered in the night air.

"You think it's true," Allie said in disbelief. "You actually believe he's Hannah's father."

Zane picked up a piece of gravel from the porch and hurled it across the yard. "I know he is."

Allie wrestled her jaw back into place. "That man isn't Hannah's father. How could you believe for one second such a ridiculous idea?"

"Kim told me he was."

CHAPTER SIX

"YOU didn't make Kim pregnant?" Allie blurted out the first thought which entered her head. "You didn't have to marry her."

"That's beside the point," Zane said in a clipped voice.

"Not to me. You dumped me for a woman who wasn't carrying your baby." Common sense asserted itself. "Except, of course, she was. Why do you suppose she lied?"

"I tried to make Kim happy. I gave her everything I could. I couldn't give her the one thing she wanted." He rubbed the back of his neck. "She wanted desperately to be loved, and I couldn't love her. I tried, but I couldn't. It was my fault. Kim wasn't a bad person. She just needed so much, and I couldn't give her what she needed. Then Hannah was born. I was in the delivery room. I took one look at her red, squalling face and tiny, perfect toes..." He stopped.

Allie could guess the rest of it. "You loved your child but didn't love her mother." She empathized with Kim Taylor's pain and despair. And bitterness. It must have eaten away at the woman watching

Zane lavish love on Hannah when Kim desperately
wanted that love for herself. For the first time Allie
saw Kim as the imperfect woman she'd been instead
of an evil monster. Pity was the last thing Allie
expected to feel for Kim Taylor.

"She was affectionate to Hannah, in a careless
sort of way. I told Kim, if she stayed home more,
she'd be less of a stranger to Hannah." He sighed
heavily. "Kim thought Hannah preferred me and
Ruth. Hell, Hannah knew who we were. I didn't
deliberately influence Hannah into preferring me."

"That must be why Kim told you the baby wasn't
yours. She was hurt and wanted to hurt back." Allie
understood that part all too well. "When did she
tell you?"

"About six months before she died. Said she'd
been pregnant when she slept with me."

"She lied. Hannah is your daughter."

"Kim named Doyle as Hannah's father," Zane
continued tonelessly. "I knew who he was, and I
thought she'd made up the story to impress me with
her actor lover, trying to make me jealous. I didn't
believe she'd slept with him."

"Whether she did or didn't, he's not Hannah's
father."

"It was like a game with Kim. She'd get mad at
me and say Hannah wasn't mine. Then she'd say
Hannah was mine and claim she'd lied in the heat
of one of our arguments." Zane punched the railing
with his fist. "I chose to believe the denials."

Moonie had come back to the porch and lain

down beside them. Now he lifted his head and whined softly. Allie leaned down and absently petted the dog. She told herself Zane didn't deserve any sympathy. "Why didn't you take a paternity test?"

"Because I don't give a damn who impregnated Kim. Hannah is my daughter."

"A paternity test would prove that."

"You don't get it, do you? One night after Kim died, I happened to see Doyle's TV program, and I saw that damned red hair, so like Hannah's. I knew then Kim hadn't lied. Not that it changed anything. I'm not giving up Hannah. I was glad Doyle wasn't interested in her." Zane pounded on the railing. "Damn, damn, damn!"

Allie tried to take pleasure in the torment in Zane's voice. Zane Peters was learning how it felt to lose control over his life. Learning how it felt to be kicked in the teeth. Learning the immense pain of losing someone you loved and the total helplessness when there wasn't a thing you could do about it.

Allie had wanted revenge. Hungered, thirsted for revenge. Required revenge.

Not in her angriest, most vengeful moment could Allie have devised a better scenario than this. Allie leaving him would never hurt him as much as losing Hannah would.

The ultimate victory. Zane Peters was finally suffering as Allie had suffered. She ought to throw back her head and crow with glee.

She couldn't. Only a monster rejoiced in this kind of pain.

Allie reached for Zane's hand. "I don't care what Kim said. Hannah is your daughter." Hannah looked too much like Zane to be anyone else's daughter. "No one is going to take her away. I don't think you have a thing to worry about."

Zane pushed away her hand. "What the hell does it matter what you think? Don't you read the damned newspapers? Kids get ripped out of their parents' arms all the time because some character claims he provided the sperm. As if being a father was nothing more than that."

"You won't lose her. Tomorrow you'll see about taking a paternity test and that will settle it."

Zane stiffened. "I'm not taking a paternity test. I'm not giving ammunition to the other side in a fight for my daughter."

Now wasn't the best time to point out he had no choice. "You can't do anything tonight, so come to bed."

"Forget it. I'm not in the mood."

A whirlwind of emotions had stormed through Allie the past few days, leaving her battered and confused. Zane's words lit on raw nerves. "As if I am! You're facing what you believe is the biggest crisis in your life, and you think I'm so shallow, I don't care about anything but having sex?"

"I didn't say that."

"Explain to me exactly what you're not in the mood for."

"Never mind. I'm not thinking too clearly right now." Zane reached out and pulled her to him. He rested his forehead on the top of her head for the merest fraction of a second before stepping back. "I'm sorry."

Her anger dissipated. Zane could hardly be held accountable for anything he said in his present state. Allie considered her options. She could walk away from Zane. Refuse to help him. Rejoice in his suffering. Or she could forget about revenge until this issue about Hannah was settled. Memories of Zane putting Hannah to bed the night she'd broken her arm made the choice easy.

"I think you need to go upstairs to bed and get a good night's sleep so tomorrow we can look at this mess with clear minds. We have to stop Sean Doyle before Hannah gets hurt."

Eventually Zane said, "You're right. I'll call my lawyer in the morning. Let's go in."

Upstairs, Allie went into the bathroom to prepare for bed. When she came out, Zane stood in Hannah's bedroom doorway. Allie moved to his side, the wooden floor cold beneath her bare feet.

Zane didn't look at her. "She's so young and innocent."

"You're doing a wonderful job raising her."

"She makes it easy."

He walked quietly away. Moonie had curled up in his dog bed at the foot of Hannah's bed. Hannah had insisted the greyhound sleep in her room, and Moonie, who'd obviously appointed himself

Hannah's protector, had not objected. Allie wondered if Zane had noticed the shine of cat eyes from
near Hannah's feet. Amber stared unblinkingly at
Allie. It appeared Hannah had two self-appointed
guardian angels.

Thunder grumbled in the distance, and a vague
uneasiness prickled Allie's spine. A nebulous men-
ace seemed to hover in the dark shadows of the hall.
Allie hugged herself, rubbing her arms. She was
imagining bogeymen where none existed. If she felt
anything at all, it was the electricity in the air in
advance of the approaching thunderstorm.

She'd let Zane's fears get to her. Of course he
was Hannah's natural father. One had only to look
at the two of them. Hannah's eyes were a lighter
blue than Zane's, but she had her father's dark eyebrows with their slight triangular peaks, and her
lashes were every bit as long and dark and thick.
Hannah's smile was an exact copy of Zane's. Zane
was definitely Hannah's father. Definitely.

The thunder clapped again, no closer. Maybe the
storm would bypass them.

Zane was in bed when Allie went to his bedroom.
Before he could say anything, she said, "I'm not
sleeping on that water bed under those mirrors, and
if you say one word to me about not wanting sex,
I swear, Zane Peters, I'll sic Moonie on you." Allie
snapped off the bedroom lights and pulled the cover
over her. "So be quiet and go to sleep."

For a long time the only sounds in the bedroom
were the sounds of their breathing, the curtains rus-

tling in the open window, and the distant thunder. Then Zane's agonized voice came out of the darkness. "It would kill me if I lost Hannah."

Allie couldn't turn away from a person's pain. Not even when that person was Zane Peters. Besides, wasn't she supposed to be pretending to be the perfect wife? Sliding across the bed, she put her arms around him, pressing against his back. "You're not going to lose her," Allie said. His torment would bring tears to a granite rock. Feeling bad for Zane meant nothing. Nor did the huge lump in her throat. "Hannah is your daughter and she'll always be your daughter. Kim lied," Allie added fiercely, her arms squeezing him, as if she could force him to believe her. "Hannah looks exactly like a Peters."

After a while, Zane said in a low voice, "Thank you."

"You'd see it yourself if you looked in the mirror."

"No, I meant for not being furious with me. I should have told you what Kim said before I married you. I don't deserve your support." He must have heard the slight sound she made, because he quickly added, "I realize you're supporting me for Hannah's sake. I know how you feel about me, and well—" he took her hand and pressed a light kiss on the back "—thank you."

Allie made no response. Resting her cheek against Zane's warm back, she lay still, willing him to fall asleep. Awake long after the threatened storm changed direction and moved off, she charted the progress of the moon across the sky each time the breeze parted the curtains.

She'd been in love with Zane Peters for years. Five years ago, hate had driven out love. She'd fed on that hate, nurtured it, until hatred gave birth to revenge.

In the wake of Zane's revelations, faced with his suffering, Allie realized revenge was not for her. Zane could suffer all the tortures of the damned, and nothing about Allie's life would change. Not the past. Not the present. Not the future.

A feeling of being rudderless took hold. It was as if, without love, without hate, without revenge, she no longer had a purpose. Zane was no longer the center of her life. No longer the focus of her emotions.

She wondered if she'd ever really loved him. She'd been young. He'd been handy, available, sexy and a good catch. Zane had easily swept her off her feet. She'd fallen in love with being in love. It wasn't until they were engaged that she began testing Zane, searching for similarities between him and Beau.

After Zane married Kim, it had been easier to dwell on hating him than to open herself up to a new relationship. She'd decided Zane and her father had taught her all she needed to know about the pain of rejection. Not caring made life safer. Especially when hate and anger filled any voids.

Only now the hate and anger had gone, and Allie

had nothing with which to replace them. What she had was an empty marriage for one month and a child who wasn't hers.

The uneven sound of his breathing told her Zane found sleep as elusive as she did. His body heated her through her pajamas. He wore nothing but undershorts. She couldn't deny she liked having her body cradle his. She liked the smell of him, the feel of his shoulder blade against her cheek.

Her reaction to him in bed last night had taken her completely by surprise. Allie had never thought of herself as a passionate woman. Once she would have called her reaction love. Older and wiser, Allie knew it for what it really was. Lust. Chemistry. Call it what one would. A lonely man. A lonely woman. Neither repulsive. Naturally there would be a certain physical attraction between them.

Not love.

Maybe love didn't even exist.

Cheyenne and Thomas thought it did. Allie smiled wryly. They were so goony about each other, they didn't count.

Her mother believed in love. Her mother probably still believed storks brought babies, too.

In the distance an owl hooted. A lonely sound. Allie's eyesight blurred and she closed her eyes. Sleep didn't come.

The filly's ears whipped in the direction of a motor vehicle screeching to a halt in front of the ranch house. Losing her concentration, the paint spooked at the gunnysack in Allie's hand and exploded in the middle of the round pen, humping her back, kicking her back legs and squealing. Allie mentally cursed the idiot who'd carelessly raced into the yard, and redoubled her efforts to desensitize the filly to such terrors as flapping blankets. The session over, Allie firmly rubbed the paint's neck and shoulders before releasing the filly into the pasture.

Now she would deal with the visitor. The idiot should never have been issued a driver's license. What if Hannah had been playing in the yard, or one of the animals dozing in the sun?

An expensive sports car with rental license plates stood in front of the house. A man ran down the porch steps and started in Allie's direction, the low-riding sun highlighting his red hair. Hanging her coil of rope over a post, Allie wished she were anywhere but here.

"May I help you?" she called, walking toward the house.

"I'm looking for Peters. Or Hannah." An appreciative gaze swept over Allie. "But you'll do."

"I'm Zane's wife. We met briefly in the bar the other evening." Allie saw no reason to explain Zane had taken Hannah with him while he ran errands.

The actor held out his hand. "Yes, I remember. I'm Sean Doyle."

Allie looked at him.

Sean Doyle dropped his hand and gave her a boyishly charming smile. "I suppose Zane told you I'm Hannah's father."

Allie was not charmed. "He told me you said you were Hannah's father. You're not. Zane is Hannah's father."

The actor gave her a sideways glance from his baby blues and said with practiced diffidence, "Kimmie and I had this thing going, if you know what I mean. She told me I was the kid's father. She slept with Peters to make me jealous and force me to marry her." He followed Allie back onto the porch.

"Why didn't you?" She sat in one of the porch chairs, having no intention of inviting him inside the house. Ruth had put dinner in the oven and gone home. No one else was around.

"I was already married, had two kids."

Allie gazed coolly at him, unimpressed by his naughty little boy smile. "I see."

He leaned forward and said earnestly, "Listen, fans don't care about a little extracurricular activity as long as a man meets his obligations. I can live with that. It's not like I sleep with every bimbo who knocks on my hotel door, and believe me, I have plenty of opportunity to mess around. The thing is, I was fond of Kimmie. I would have given her money for support if she hadn't married Peters."

Allie almost felt sorry for him. One day his boy-ish good looks would fade and he'd have nothing inside to fall back on. "Mr. Doyle," she said quietly, "Hannah's not your child."

"Call me Sean. Kimmie said she was."

Allie swallowed the words that Kim Taylor had

lied. "Hold your little fingers together. Like this." Palms facing her, Allie lined up her two little fingers.

Giving her a bewildered look, the actor copied her action.

"Your fingers touch each other all the way to the tips."

"So? Everyone's does," he said.

She shook her head. "Zane's don't. They drastically curve away from each other. So do his mother's. She told me once her mother's curved the same way, as did her grandfather's. Zane's sister's fingers curve that way." Allie paused for effect. "Hannah's fingers curve exactly like her father's."

"Fingers don't prove anything. Probably half the people in the world have curving fingers. I'm getting a lawyer, and going to court and getting my daughter."

"Why are you doing this?"

"Nobody's going to call me a deadbeat father."

He'd waited over four years to consider that. Allie wondered how much the Taylors had influenced him. "Go back to California and be a father to your own children."

"My wife won't let me. She and her fancy lawyer claimed I'm not a good father. I can only see them one weekend a month. When I take Kimmie's kid back, Jessie—that's my wife—she'll see I can be a good father."

"You're not Hannah's father," Allie said, gentler than she intended. Zane drove through the gate and headed around to the back of the barn. He wouldn't be happy about Sean Doyle coming here. Allie stood, eager to get rid of their unwanted visitor. "Pursuing this is a waste of time and money."

"I don't care what it costs," he said stubbornly. "I have plenty of money."

Allie sighed, impatient with bullheaded, stupid men. She'd wanted to tell Zane first, but this business had to be stopped before Hannah got hurt. "Mr. Doyle, Sean, I made some phone calls today. There's a simple DNA test which will prove you absolutely cannot be Hannah's father. It's painless and discreet. Your fans won't need to know anything about it."

"You mean have them take blood for a paternity test?"

"You don't need blood for a DNA test. It would prove conclusively you are not Hannah's father." He wasn't. She knew he wasn't. The red hair was a coincidence. It had to be.

"Allie's here." Hannah shouted from the back seat of the pickup. Zane had already spotted Allie's SUV parked near the house. His wife's car. He liked thinking that. Liked knowing she was home. Liked having her in his bed. He wished he'd made love to her last night. The way she'd immediately rallied to support him gave him a hopeful feeling.

Parking behind the barn, Zane opened the truck door. Moonie bounded out, then waited for Hannah who extracted herself from her car seat and launched into Zane's arms. He squeezed her briefly, then held her out in front of him, trying to see his sister or his mother in her. To him, Hannah looked like Hannah. He scrutinized her face. Blue eyes laughed at him. Were they his blue eyes?

He hadn't been able to reach his lawyer this morning. The attorney had been scheduled for court all day. Zane would talk to him tomorrow. Lawyers earned their money for stuff like getting rid of Doyle. Zane would pay whatever it took, do whatever he had to do to convince Doyle to drop the matter. Doyle had known for over four years he'd supposedly fathered Kim's child and had done nothing. Surely that negated his parental rights. Zane could adopt Hannah. He wouldn't let her go.

Hannah swung her legs. "Put me down, Daddy. Moonie and I gotta go tell Honey we're back."

"Stay out of the pasture," Zane warned. "No farther than the fence. You or Moonie."

"Okay." Hannah skipped through the open barn and across the yard, Moonie gamboling at her heels.

Zane watched the pair for a minute, then headed for the house. Hannah would follow orders. He wanted to see his wife. The minute he'd turned in the gate, he'd seen she wasn't alone, but shadows had hidden her visitor's identity from him.

He hadn't recognized the sports car. Probably Steele's. Cheyenne must be here.

When he was married to Kim, Zane never knew who he'd find at the house when he came home.

Kim accused him of spying on her. It saddened him that he hadn't cared enough to spy.

He heard the voices before he reached the porch. Allie's and a man's low mumble.

Fragments of Allie's conversation carried clearly. "DNA test...prove conclusively you...Hannah's father."

Zane froze, blindsided by her words. Last night, when the bottom of his world had dropped out, Allie had lent him her strength, given him her immediate and undivided loyalty.

Loyalty. What loyalty? A red mist of rage shimmered before him as the explanation for her duplicitous behavior hit him.

Revenge. The woman he'd once thought one of the most caring in the world had become this person he no longer knew.

An iron vise painfully squeezed his chest. Hurting him was one thing, but for Allie to use Hannah as an instrument of her revenge was monstrous.

Zane clenched his jaw and strode up the porch stairs. Two startled faces turned toward him. So busy plotting their nasty little surprise, they hadn't heard his approach. "Get out of here, Doyle, before I throw you out."

Allie moved to Zane's side and laid her hand on his arm. "I think you and Sean should talk."

They were already on a cozy, first-name basis. Zane hadn't thought he could get angrier. He could. Flinging off her hand, he said to the actor, "You heard me. Get off my place."

Doyle edged away. "Allie said we should get paternity tests."

"My wife," Zane said tightly, "says a lot of things. I don't need a damned paternity test to know Hannah is my daughter. Get out and stay out and keep away from my daughter." He would have added keep away from his wife, except his wife had already sided with the enemy. Zane wouldn't think about that now. He refused to let her know how deep her betrayal cut.

They silently watched the actor get into his car. Zane's mind raced furiously. He'd get a restraining order. He didn't even know what the hell a restraining order did, but he sure as hell was going to get one. He'd alert Ruth and the men to be extraprotective of Hannah, to watch for Doyle. They'd start locking the gate.

He couldn't bring himself to look at Allie. He wouldn't give her a key. She could honk for admission like everyone else who didn't belong on the place. Hell no, he wanted her gone.

Before he could open his mouth, Hannah ran toward the porch.

"We'll wait until after she goes to bed to discuss this," Allie said calmly.

As if she hadn't buried her revengeful knife up to the hilt in his back. The only thing they had to discuss was how long it would take her to pack.

"Allie," Hannah cried, "Daddy got me and Moonie ice cream."

Allie put her hands on her hips. "Where's mine?" she demanded playfully.

The two-faced…pretending she didn't hate the little girl running toward her. Allie had laid out her feelings at the hospital. His mistake was in not believing her. He hadn't wanted to believe her.

He'd wanted to sleep with her.

She bent over, saying something to Hannah. Her jeans hugged the curves of her bottom. Zane's jaw ached.

He still wanted to sleep with her.

Allie put down the travel magazine at the sound of Zane's footsteps. "She settled down for the night?"

"In my office."

The snapped order annoyed her, but she reminded herself Zane was under a lot of stress. Following him into his office, Allie dropped into the worn, overstuffed chair in front of his desk. "You don't have to bite off my nose," she said mildly.

He stood looking out of the uncurtained window, his back to her. "You haven't moved much stuff in. Obviously you knew you wouldn't be staying long. Thirty minutes should give you enough time to pack up and leave. Forget about your mare. I'll trailer her to the Double Nickel in the morning."

Stunned, Allie stared at his rigid back. "What are you talking about? I'm not going anywhere."

Zane banged his knuckles against the wooden windowsill. "I only have one question. Was it just a lucky break for you when Vern and Edie dug up

Doyle, or were you in on it from the beginning of our marriage?''

The fury in his voice jolted her as much as the astonishing question. ''Until last night, I didn't even know Kim and Sean were acquainted.''

''Then you must have danced for joy when you heard my pathetic tale.'' Turning, Zane centered a burning stare on her. ''Congratulations. You've always been good at hiding your feelings, but last night proved how expert you've become.''

She crossed her arms in front of her. ''What exactly are you accusing me of, Zane?''

''Cut the innocent act. It won't work. I know why you married me.''

He couldn't know. She held his gaze. ''Why?''

''Revenge,'' he said flatly. ''Don't bother denying it.''

So he had guessed. ''All right. I won't.''

''Damn you, Allie,'' he said wearily. ''I don't blame you for hating me, but did you have to include Hannah in your revenge?''

''I'm not exactly sure what you think I've done,'' she said slowly, ''but I never intended to hurt Hannah, only you.''

''The woman scorned,'' he said bitterly. ''I never thought you'd be a damned walking cliché.''

''I never thought I'd be dumped before my wedding,'' Allie flashed. ''That's a pretty crummy cliché, too.''

''I know what I did to you was unforgivable. I guessed why you married me, but I never believed you were capable of hurting Hannah to get back at me. That's what comes from thinking with what's below my belt instead of using my brains."

"A common problem with you," she snapped. How could he think she'd harm Hannah?

"I suppose you think I deserve to lose the daughter I dumped you for."

Allie lowered her anger to a slow simmer. Zane Peters was going to get a piece of her mind, a big piece, but first she had to find out why he'd suddenly concluded this whole mess was her fault. "Did you ever reach your lawyer today?" The question merited an icy look of contempt. She tried again. "I made some phone calls."

"I'll just bet you did."

She took a deep breath. "I remembered reading in the newspaper about a place that does DNA testing. I went to the library, found the article and called their 800 number. It's fast and discreet. All you have to do is scrape the inside of your mouth with a cotton swab and mail it to them. We can send them samples from you and Hannah and Sean."

"I'm not taking any damned paternity test and neither is Hannah."

"Zane, use your head. It's the best way to get rid of Sean. The tests will prove he's not the father, one hundred percent for sure, and that you are, with a ninety-nine or something like that percent certainty. No one else could match Hannah that close unless you had a brother who'd slept with Kim."

Zane stalked over to her chair. Looming over her,

he gripped the chair's arms. "You told me to look in the mirror. I looked. Hannah's hair, the small nose, the soft chin. None of that comes from me or Kim."

"She's four years old and she's a girl. Of course she has a soft chin and a small nose." Allie didn't know why she bothered. She couldn't reach him. Couldn't convince him.

She refused to give up. "If I'm wrong about the tests, then we'll fight for Hannah. You've raised Hannah while Sean ignored her. She loves you. We'll get psychiatrists' reports, testimonials to what a good father you are, whatever it takes. We'll bury the judge under a blizzard of papers."

"Do you ever read the newspapers?" he snarled. "Courts don't give a damn about all that. They haul off a hysterical child and pat themselves on the back for a job well-done."

Allie refused to back down. Not when she knew she was right. She had to be right. "I don't know why you want to believe Hannah isn't your child." His head jerked back as if she'd slugged him. His eyes darkened with pain. Allie forced herself to continue. "You can't drag Kim's name through the mud. She is Hannah's mother. But if you don't voluntarily take a paternity test, Sean will go to court, and everything will be a matter of public record. Is that what you want?"

"I want you to mind your own business," he bit out.

"Think about Hannah. What if she'd been outside playing when Sean arrived? What if he'd told her he was her father? Are you willing to risk putting Hannah through that? The courts will force you to take the test. Take it now and get it over with so you can get on with your life.''

Zane's eyes narrowed. ''Doyle didn't know about this wonderful little service until you told him.''

''Is that why you're mad at me? Get your head out of the sand, Zane. 'DNA tests' probably would have been the first words out of any high-priced lawyer's mouth.''

''You don't know that. I would have refused.''

He knew he couldn't refuse. Allie read the knowledge on his face before Zane swung away from her and returned to his post by the window.

Standing, Allie took a piece of paper out of her pocket and laid it on Zane's desk. ''Here's the phone number of the DNA testing place and Sean's phone number. He's staying in Aspen.'' Before exiting his office, she paused. ''I know you're worried about Hannah, so for now I'll ignore your accusations. Once the test results are back, we'll have to talk.''

He pivoted on his heel to face her. ''Where are you going?''

''Taking Moonie out. I don't care how much you rant and rave, I'm not leaving until this is settled.''

''And when it is?'' he asked tightly.

''I don't know.'' She took a step and stopped, adding over her shoulder, ''I do know I'm not sleeping on that water bed. If you don't want to share a bed with me, you sleep on it. Or sleep on the floor or on the living room sofa. I'm sleeping in your bed with or without you. You strong-armed me into marrying you, and the least you can do is let me have a good night's sleep.''

Zane slept on the sofa in the living room. In the morning Allie folded his sheets and blankets and put them away before Ruth came. Each evening Zane dragged them out of the linen closet again and silently made the sofa into a bed.

Aimlessly tapping her pencil on the top of the table, Allie hoped he slept as little as she did.

She should never have married Zane. Not even for a month.

For much of her life, Allie had believed marriage to Zane would make life perfect. She'd married him, and life was far from perfect. They were two strangers living in the same house. Polite, but distant. If it weren't for Hannah, Allie doubted Zane would show up at the dinner table. Or come home at all. He'd shut Allie completely out of his life.

Not that she cared. She hadn't wanted to marry him.

He had not touched her since their wedding night.

How could he believe Allie capable of something so heinous as plotting to make him lose Hannah?

Allie had practically promised him she'd stay a month, but his accusations canceled any implied promise. She couldn't come up with a single reason why she should stay one more minute.

"How come Daddy doesn't have to go to bed?" Sitting quietly at the table drawing pictures, Hannah startled Allie with her sudden question.

"He goes to bed." Allie hadn't realized the little girl was aware of their sleeping arrangements.

Hannah shook her head. "He makes me go to bed so I'm not grumpy. Daddy's grumpy."

Trust a child to sense the tension Zane tried to hide. Fighting hard to keep Hannah unaware of the drama swirling around her, Zane's efforts obviously had the opposite effect. "When grown-ups worry about things, they sound kind of grumpy."

"How come Daddy's worried?"

Allie scrambled for a suitable answer. "Grown-ups worry about everything."

"I'm not gonna be a grown-up."

"Wise move, honey."

Hannah stopped scribbling on her cast with a red crayon and fixed a bright, inquisitive look on Allie. "How come you called me honey? Daddy calls me honey. He loves me. How come Daddy doesn't call you honey? Davy said Daddy loves you. Davy said that's why you got married."

Since Hannah had stayed in Hope Valley the night of her father's wedding, Allie had been treated to a mind-boggling array of Davy's opinions. "Davy doesn't know what he's talking about," she said sharply.

"Does, too," Hannah said defiantly. After a minute she added in a mutinous little voice, "Davy's a big kid. He knows everything." She didn't look at

Allie, but bent over a piece of paper, concentrating on her drawing.

Allie tried to work, but guilt for snapping at Hannah nagged at her. There was nothing she could do to convince Zane he was wrong about her. Allie didn't even care to try. She could, however, for the short duration of her marriage try to make life easier for Hannah while Zane battled his demons. Allie set out to make amends. "What are you drawing?"

Hannah kept her head down. "A picture."

"Of what?"

"People."

"May I see?"

Hannah hesitated before pushing the sheet of paper across the table. White space separated three stick figures. The largest figure had black hair. The middle-size one had yellow hair. Red circles surrounded the smallest figure's head. All three figures had black half circles for mouths. The mouths turned down.

"Tell me about the picture," Allie said.

Hannah ripped the paper wrap off a black crayon. "They look unhappy."

Hannah shrugged.

"I wonder how we can make them happy," Allie mused.

Hannah stopped fiddling with her crayon. After a long moment, she peeked up at Allie. "Ice cream?"

Every time he saw her drive away, Zane wondered if this would be the day Allie didn't return.

He told himself she wouldn't leave without her mare, then he remembered he'd brought the mare over in his trailer. Allie would send Worth for Copper.

The small of his back ached. He was damned sick and tired of sleeping on the sofa. The bed belonged to him. He ought to take her up on her challenge, crawl into bed beside her. See how long it took before she fled to another room.

The hell of it was, what if she didn't flee? He'd be lying close to her warm body, within reach of her silken skin. He knew where one touch would lead.

How could he want to sleep with her after she'd betrayed him?

He wanted to trust her. If only she hadn't admitted she wanted revenge. Not that he hadn't guessed her intentions when she married him. He hadn't guessed she'd use Hannah as her instrument of revenge.

Zane halted his truck behind the barn and rested his head on his arms against the steering wheel. In hindsight, Allie's intent was crystal clear. Hell, his mother packed more when she came to visit for a week than Allie had brought to the house. Allie had never intended to stay married to him.

If only he hadn't made love to her on their wedding night. A man didn't miss what he'd never known.

He'd come so close to attaining his long-time dream of marriage to Allie. She'd made a mockery of his dream. Destroyed the love he'd once felt for her.

He'd never love again. Wasn't that enough for Allie? Did she have to make him lose Hannah, too?

He'd never thought the day would come when he hated Allie Lassiter.

CHAPTER SEVEN

WALKING into the cool, shadowed hallway of his ranch house, Zane felt the emptiness. His heart skipped a beat before he remembered seeing Allie's SUV parked out front. Listening, he heard only silence. Although he could smell dinner cooking, Ruth must have gone home. Faint laughter came from the screened porch off the kitchen. He walked down the long hallway, stopping at the screened door to the porch.

Allie sat sprawled in an old, beat-up relic of a club chair, her feet propped on a footstool. Hannah knelt near the stool, her back to Zane.

"I don't think he would," Allie said.

"Daddy would," Hannah insisted.

Zane pushed open the door. "Daddy would what?"

"Daddy!" Hannah squealed, and rushed toward him. Once the pain had eased, she'd quickly adjusted to the cast on her left arm. Holding a small bottle in her left hand, she waved a tiny brush with her right.

The smell hit him as Allie urged caution on Hannah. "What are you doing?" he asked.

"Look, Daddy!"

Zane followed Hannah's gaze downward to her wiggling toes. Cute round toes with bright orange toenails.

"Allie did 'em, and I'm doing hers."

Zane glanced at Allie. She smiled. He immediately grew wary. Forcing his gaze from her damned kissable lips, he looked where Hannah pointed. Lavender polish smeared the tops of most of Allie's toes.

"Aren't they beautiful?" Hannah asked proudly. "I can paint yours, too."

"Well, um…"

Allie laughed. "See? I told you men don't appreciate beautiful toes."

Zane appreciated beautiful toes. An image flashed across his mind. Allie sprawled, not on the chair, but on his bed. He'd never before ached to make love to a woman's toes.

"How come you don't like painted toenails, Daddy?" Hannah bent over Allie's foot, studiously globbing paint on the top of a bare toe.

"I like painted toenails, but on girls, not on me."

"Allie's not a girl. She's old."

"Old!" Allie echoed in mock indignation. "If I'm old, your father is ancient."

Zane's gaze flashed to her face and his breath caught at the look she gave him. The warm, intimate kind adults shared when children did something cute or funny. He wondered what trickery hid behind her smiles. Masking his suspicious thoughts with a slight smile, he addressed Hannah's remarks. "I meant men don't wear toenail polish, like we don't wear dresses."

"We're not wearing dresses," Hannah said.

Zane didn't need his daughter to point out the obvious. From the moment he'd joined them, he'd been aware of Allie's lightly tanned, long, shapely legs. She had no business wearing shorts that short in September. No business tempting him to run his hands over her bare skin.

"Allie, I made another boo-boo," Hannah wailed.

"It's okay. A little polish remover will fix it."

"We're gonna be pretty for our party, Daddy."

Images of his legs entwined with Allie's vanished. "What party?"

"We're gonna have ice cream," Hannah said happily. "Davy's coming and everybody."

"Just family," Allie said. "They're coming over Sunday."

"Ruth doesn't work on Sundays."

"I know. We'll barbecue. Everyone's bringing something."

"Everyone?"

"Mom and Worth and Greeley. And Cheyenne and Thomas."

"And Davy," Hannah said in an anxious voice.

Allie smiled at his daughter. "Of course, Davy. And we'll ask Grandma and Grandpa Taylor."

White-hot anger flashed through Zane as he realized where her smiles and tricks were leading. "I suppose you've sent an engraved invitation to Doyle," he said tightly.

"I told you," Allie said, "we're just having family."

How could Allie think about having a damned party when his life was disintegrating? If she had the least shred of decency, felt the least bit of kindness toward Hannah, she wouldn't be planning a celebration. Not now.

Unless she was celebrating victory. He'd mailed in the damned swabs for the DNA test. He knew what the outcome would be, but waiting for the test results gave him a little breathing room. Time to plan. Maybe hire a private investigator to dig into Doyle's life. If he had to resort to blackmail to keep Hannah, he would.

Losing Hannah didn't bear thinking about.

Zane opened the closet door and reached for a blanket, then stopped. Damn it. Why should he sleep on the sofa? The house, the bed, belonged to him. Allie had destroyed his life. There was no reason she should destroy his back. Closing the door he marched down the hall toward the bedroom. His bedroom.

Allie looked up as he threw open his bedroom door. "It occurred to me, I should have asked you a crucial question about Sunday before I started issuing invitations."

He scowled at her. "Just one?"

"I'm sure more will come to me." She returned

her attention to the pad in her hand. "The question is, can you grill?"

"What?" He didn't exactly know what question he'd braced himself to hear, but that wasn't it.

"Grill. You know? Cook outdoors on a barbecue grill? No matter what Worth puts on the grill, what he takes off is raw or charcoal briquettes, and I suspect Thomas has never barbecued in his life. So the crucial question is, can you grill?"

"Allie," he began, then hesitated. How did a man go about discussing his wife's treachery when she insisted on talking about something as mundane as cooking?

"I know, I know. It's sexist, expecting the man of the house to do the barbecuing, but for Hannah's sake, I'd like the party to go well, even if it's just family."

"Allie," he tried again.

"The thing is, Worth is a closet chauvinist when it comes to barbecuing. He thinks it's a man's job. Whenever Mom or I or Cheyenne or Greeley planned to grill, he insisted on doing it. Not wanting to hurt his feelings, we let him, but he is, without a doubt, the worst outdoor chef in the state of Colorado. If he sees me grilling, he'll take over. If you grill, he'll stand around and talk cows and sports, the way guys always do."

"I can handle the grill."

"Good." Allie wrote something, then studied her pad.

What the hell was going on? Zane hadn't felt so

disoriented since he'd awakened five years ago to find himself in Kim Taylor's bed. A few days ago Allie had vilely betrayed him, and now apparently all she had on her mind was a barbecue. If he'd left a movie for popcorn and come back into the theater to find a different movie playing, he couldn't be more befuddled.

She looked up from her pad. "What do you want?"

He wanted her under him.

The sudden heat of desire jolted him. Allie had betrayed him, sabotaged his life, and he wanted to bury himself in her warmth. How could he even think of warmth in connection with Allie after what she'd done? His weakness angered him. Wanting Allie was a betrayal of Hannah.

Allie didn't wait for his answer. "I thought steaks, but if you'd rather fix hamburgers, I don't care. I promised Hannah we'd have hot dogs, too."

She'd been asking about the damned barbecue.

"Mom is bringing a chocolate cake. Cheyenne said they'll hit the deli, and Greeley is making her famous potato salad. Hannah and I can make bread, unless you want to fix hamburgers, then I'll buy buns. Let's see." She jotted on the pad. "Condiments, lemonade, iced tea and baked beans. You always liked my grandmother's baked bean recipe. Ice cream, of course. Can you think of anything else?"

He wanted to tell her to quit acting. Allie had always excelled at hiding her feelings, but he'd never seen her put on a performance this remarkable. If he didn't know better, he'd think they were a normal married couple discussing the trivia of their lives as they prepared for bed.

The hell with her games. He could play a few games himself. "I'm not sleeping on that damned sofa anymore."

"Okay." She didn't look up.

Damn her. "This is my house and my bed, and I'm sleeping here whether you like it or not."

Her nostrils briefly flared with annoyance. "Sleep where you want."

"I intend to." Zane sat on the edge of the bed and pulled off his boots. Standing, he yanked off his shirt. His hands went to the waistband of his jeans. Allie hadn't moved. "Well?" He waited for her to dash from the room. He didn't give a damn where she slept.

Allie looked at him. Her eyes darkened. "Well, what?"

It didn't take an advanced degree in psychology to interpret the flushed look on her face. However Allie had meant the question, the voice she'd asked it in had been low and sensuous. Less question than sultry challenge.

Zane's body hardened. Her need for revenge had killed any love he'd had for her. She meant nothing to him. That didn't mean he couldn't use her. Maybe find forgetfulness for a short time. His gaze holding hers, Zane unfastened his jeans, leaving them to hang on his hips as he rounded the foot of the bed. Reaching down, he took the pad and pencil from her loose grasp and set them on the bedside table, then snapped off the lamp. His jeans hit the floor with a muffled thump. Allie said nothing as he slid into bed and reached for her.

Allie dumped sugar into the pitcher of lemonade and stirred vigorously. Pretending for Hannah's sake that things were normal didn't mean a person had to enjoy herself enthusiastically in the marital bed. Blame Zane. Allie could control her reactions better if he were an unsatisfactory lover. Except of course, what they did had nothing to do with love. Zane wanted sex and an escape from reality. Allie knew he was using her to hold his fears temporarily at bay.

Why not? She was using him to... Well, actually, Allie didn't know why she was using him. When she tried to analyze her behavior in Zane's bed, her thoughts got stuck on inconsequential details such as the width of Zane's shoulders, the warmth of his skin, his heart beating against her palms. It was sick. When a woman felt totally neutral toward a man, her stomach shouldn't turn squishy funny at the sight of his bare chest.

Worse was admitting she liked listening to his steady breathing at her side as he slept. She liked seeing the false dawn in the sky and hearing the early bird song as his hands molded her to him again.

She liked everything about being married to Zane. Except being married to him.

She'd gone stark raving mad.

In the oven a pot of baked beans slowly bubbled. Bread cooled on racks. The freezer held three flavors of ice cream, and steaks and iced tea waited in the refrigerator. Allie had come downstairs to take care of last-minute preparations while Zane supervised Hannah's bath.

Allie's stirring slowed. Funny how a woman could plan to marry a man and have his children and never consider what kind of father he'd make. Years ago Allie had seen Zane as strong and handsome and sexy. Seeing him with Hannah disclosed qualities she'd never considered. Strength, yes, but gentleness and firmness. He protected and nurtured his daughter, and Hannah adored him.

"No! I don't wanna! I don't like you, Daddy! I'm gonna tell Allie!" Hannah yelled from the upper floor, then ran down the staircase and down the hall, calling for Allie. The little girl charged into the kitchen, her mouth turned dramatically downward. "Daddy said I hafta put on shoes!"

"Is that what you're wearing?" Allie asked, looking in disbelief at the seemingly ubiquitous neon pink dress.

Hannah pirouetted. "It's my party dress." Pressing the ruffled skirt to her knees, she looked down at feet encased in white patent leather shoes. "They can't see my pretty toes!" she wailed. "Tell Daddy I can't put on shoes."

"Well, uh..." A sound alerted her and Allie looked up to see Zane lean against the kitchen door-jamb. He lifted an eyebrow and waited.

Allie took a deep breath and started with the dress. "Since it's a barbecue party, your father and I are wearing jeans."

"Wanna wear my party dress," Hannah said mulishly.

Allie took another look at the atrocious dress. "All right." With luck Hannah would destroy it. "Put on your sandals and your toenails will show."

Zane folded his arms across his chest. "She doesn't have sandals. She lives on a ranch. It's boots or her white shoes."

Allie looked at father and daughter. One challenging face and one expectant face stared back. Great. Now she knew how Solomon felt rendering judgments. Allie wanted to smack both their knuckles with the lemonade spoon. She wasn't anyone's mother. Why were they looking at her? "Okay, here's the deal, Hannah. Wear your cowboy boots—"

"*Noooo!*"

"Let me finish. Boots when you're off the porch, but you can go barefoot in the house or on the porch."

"Okay." Hannah sat on the floor and tugged at her shoes.

"I'm not through. If you don't put your boots on when you leave the porch, then you may not go barefoot anymore."

"Okay." Holding her shoes and stockings, Hannah stood and smirked at Zane. "See, Daddy," she said smugly, "I tol' ya. Allie knows 'cause she's a big lady."

Zane lightly swatted his daughter's behind as she trotted past him to get her boots. "Show a little respect for your father."

Hannah came running back. "I love you," she said seriously, "but you don't know about pretty toes."

"I know about toes. In fact, I just might eat yours with mustard and ketchup at our party."

"No!" Hannah squealed with delight. "I'm gonna eat yours!" Giggling she ran from the room.

The laughter on Zane's face faded, and his shoulders slumped.

Clearing her throat, Allie said, "I don't know why I bothered to fix beans if everyone's eating toes for dinner."

Zane squared his shoulders and brought his gaze to rest on her face. "A good question. Why did you bother?"

She almost blurted out because he liked them. "You give a party, you have to have food."

"Why give a party? To celebrate what a sap I was to marry you?"

Allie traded spoons and opened the oven to stir the beans. "You might recall whose idea this dumb marriage was." She slammed the oven door. And remembered she'd mentioned marriage first. Which Zane would no doubt quickly remind her.

"Allie." Zane's hands clamped on her shoulders. "How'd we come to this? I never wanted to fight with you, but it drove me crazy the way you assumed I was like Beau."

Her fingers curled painfully around the spoon. "Don't put the blame on me. I'm not the one who slept with someone else."

His hands fell away. "It always comes down to that, doesn't it?"

Allie whirled. "What do you expect? You betrayed me."

His face utterly still, Zane stared down at her.

Allie took a deep breath. "There's no point rehashing the past." Gripping the spoon, she turned to face the sink. "The steaks are in the refrigerator. Have you started the grill?"

"It's gas."

Allie stared out the window at a chipmunk eating dandelion seed heads. She wished Zane would leave the kitchen. Thinking of what might have been hurt too much. The drawn-out silence behind her vibrated with tension. Just leave. The unspoken prayer seemed to bounce off the cupboards and walls.

Zane moved to stand directly behind her, his body heat bridging the space between them. "Allie." He slid his hands down her upper arms. "We could start over. We're older, wiser. We could try to make this marriage work. If you wanted."

The spoon fell from lifeless fingers into the sink. First shock, then an unexpected reaction jolted Allie. She wanted to try. She wanted to say yes.

Fear held her silent. Giving Zane her body had been easy. Trusting him meant a far greater risk. She'd barely recovered from the last time he'd hurt her. If he hurt her again...

She sensed something wonderful hovering just beyond her reach. It could be hers. All she had to do was reach out and grab it. Take a chance.

"Hello? Anyone home?"

Zane dropped his hands at the shout from the front hall and stepped back. "Forget it. It's too late for us to start over."

Allie whirled. "Zane..." The indifference in his blue eyes silenced her.

"I think our guests have arrived," he said coolly and left the room.

Leaving Allie to fail miserably at making sense of the chaos he'd made of her emotions.

She'd stood in his kitchen, in front of his stove, and Zane's ability to reason had flown out the window. He'd wanted so badly to believe his fairy tale, he'd mindlessly ignored the evidence of her betrayal, and like an idiot, suggested they stay married. No wonder Allie hadn't known how to respond. She must have been struggling to keep from laughing in his face.

Now he knew why she was giving a party. More turning the knife. His wife—inwardly he gave the label a mocking sneer—had put on a good show of surprise when she'd seen Sean Doyle with the rest of them, but she hadn't fooled Zane.

Absently Zane smoothed down Hannah's curls as she stuck to his leg. Strangers milling around paying her extravagant compliments made her bashful.

"What a beautiful dress," Doyle said in the hearty voice clueless adults use with children. "Will you come over here so I can get a better look at it?"

Hannah stuck her thumb into her mouth and shook her head.

Mary Lassiter rolled her eyeballs at Zane and held her hand out to Hannah. "Davy and I want to see Honey. Come show us which one she is."

Hannah hopped off the porch, stopped, gave Zane a guilty look and dashed back to the porch. Sitting, she thrust her bare feet into boots, one eye on Allie. Allie pretended not to notice. Or more likely, Zane thought savagely, Allie didn't give a damn if Hannah stepped in a cow pie or on a rusty nail.

Her boots on, Hannah joined Mary and Davy as they headed for the pasture fence. Mary had a way with kids. The trio had traveled barely two feet from the house before Mary and Hannah swung clasped hands as Hannah skipped and chattered.

Zane stiffened as Doyle stood. He was damned if he'd let the actor pester Hannah.

"Sean, come here and help us out." Allie pointed to a chair near her. "We know half of what Jake is telling us about Hollywood is lies, but we don't know which half. We need you to tell us when he's lying."

The TV actor eagerly joined the crowd around Jake Norton.

"Finally. I've been dying to get you to myself." The dark-haired woman who'd been introduced as Jake Norton's wife sat in the chair beside Zane.

"Why?"

"Because I've long wanted to meet the man who broke Allie's heart." Kristy Norton gave him a lopsided smile. "Not exactly the most brilliant way to start a conversation, was it?"

"No."

Kristy laughed. "An honest man." She put crimson-tipped fingers on his arm. "I'm so happy for Allie. It's great the way she and your daughter adore each other."

Zane saw no reason to set her straight. She was right about Hannah, anyway.

"Although you were mean to get married without us. We were stunned when we arrived last night and Cheyenne told us. I told Jake he has to persuade you to let him use your wedding in a movie. I love that image of Allie in blue jeans." The woman studied Zane's face. "I'll bet she was a beautiful bride."

Zane's hands tightened on the arms of his chair. "Yes."

A slow smile spread over the woman's face. "I see why she never gave other men the time of day."

Zane didn't. "She has no trouble giving Doyle the time of day."

"Blame Jake for hauling Sean here today. I keep telling my husband he can't just show up at people's houses with uninvited guests." She dimpled. "Not that we aren't uninvited ourselves, but Cheyenne said we'd be a big surprise." Kristy gave Zane a shrewd look. "Not all surprises are good."

Zane found himself liking the outspoken woman. "Allie's friends are always welcome at my place."

"Jake's doing another Western movie, and Sean wants to play the second lead. He attached himself to Jake the second we ran into him in the J-Bar at the Hotel Jerome. The part would be great for his career, but I'm not sure he has the right look."

"I thought women liked Doyle's look."

"Adolescent females. He's too pretty. This movie has parts for two rough, he-man types. Like Jake and you and Worth. Your faces have the kind of hard edge that appeals to men as well as women. What do you think, Allie?" she called across the porch. "Doesn't Zane belong in pictures? He's the epitome of the strong, silent, rugged, rock-solid, dependable cowpoke. And really sexy, don't you agree?"

Allie gave Zane a startled look. "I think I heard a buzzer go off in the kitchen. I'd better check the baked beans."

Worth and Norton hooted at the notion of Zane being sexy.

He ignored them, watching Allie bolt into the house. He'd thought she'd gotten over her habit of changing the subject or running away rather than tell a lie. She certainly hadn't had any trouble look-

ing him in the eye while she uttered one falsehood
after another.

"Really, I don't need help cooking," Allie said.

Greeley herded Allie out to the back porch. "We
didn't come out to the kitchen to help you cook."

Cheyenne shut the screen door behind them.
"What's wrong?"

Well acquainted with the look on Cheyenne's
face, Allie had no hope she'd be allowed to escape.
Putting off the inevitable, she said, "Nothing's
wrong. I need to stir the beans."

"You just stirred them." Cheyenne blocked the
door. "Why the frantic summons to a party?"

"There wasn't anything frantic about it. Hannah
and I decided to give a party."

"You know once Cheyenne gets the bit in her
teeth she won't let go, so you may as well 'fess up,
Allie. Zane looks like a trainload of dynamite about
to blow up, and you're skittering around like grease
on a hot skillet. What's going on?"

Allie looked at her sisters in mingled exasperation
and affection. "We've never given a party together,
that's all."

The looks on her sisters' faces told her they had
no intention of letting her brush them off.

She capitulated. In a roundabout way. She desperately needed a second opinion. If she'd been
wrong... "Greeley, do you remember that time
when you were about ten or eleven and you came
home crying because someone said you didn't look

like Cheyenne and me? You said they meant you weren't a member of our family.''

Greeley nodded. ''I remember. Worth said I should count my blessings I didn't look like a couple of tall, skinny, blond bimbos. Cheyenne wanted to make the person apologize. You said you liked how I looked, and Mom said how I looked inside was what counted.''

''And Grandpa said we were like cattle.'' The three sisters said the words in unison and laughed.

Cheyenne shook her head. ''Grandpa always knew which calf went with which cow. He said it was a matter of knowing what to look for.''

''Mom brought out the family pictures and we studied them,'' Allie said. ''We figured out all four of us have Beau's mouth and cheekbones, that Greeley has Beau's hair and eyebrows, and the rest of us have Mom's height and coloring.''

Greeley grinned. ''Remember how mad Worth was when he realized his mouth looked like his sisters'?''

Cheyenne gave Allie a curious look. ''Why are you bringing that up now?''

''Studying other people until we could pick out in a crowd who was related to whom became a game with us. The ability came in handy when I taught. These days kids have so many stepmothers and stepdads and half siblings and stepwhatevers... Knowing what to look for kept me from making some major goofs.''

''Allie,'' Cheyenne prodded.

Allie pulled on the pot holder she held in her hand. "Zane thinks Hannah isn't his child."

"Get serious," Greeley said. "With those eyebrows? Does she have the crooked fingers?"

At Allie's nod, Cheyenne said, "Where did Zane get such a crazy idea?"

"Kim Taylor." Allie explained the whole convoluted mess.

"Once the test results come back, Zane will agree that taking them was the smart thing to do," her younger sister said.

Cheyenne gave Allie a sharp look. "What's the part you're not telling us?"

Allie shrugged. "That's pretty much it. Of course Zane is furious about Sean coming this afternoon, and it's perfectly obvious he thinks I invited Sean even though I told him I didn't." Words she hadn't intended to say rushed out. "Zane thinks I'm trying to make him lose Hannah to pay him back for marrying Kim instead of me five years ago. I admitted to him that initially I wanted revenge, but how can he think I'm capable of something so unconscionable? He says he wants me to get out, then he says he wants us to start over, then he says it's too late to start over. I never should have married him."

"It's my fault. I shouldn't have invited him to my wedding," Cheyenne said.

"We can't worry about what everyone should or shouldn't have done," Greeley said. "Allie's problem now is what to do about Zane."

"That's easy." Mary Lassiter's voice came from the other side of the screen. "Just shoot him."

Allie jumped. "Mom. How long have you been standing there?"

"Long enough to know if Zane were a horse, you'd tell his owner to put him down."

"I have never ever told an owner to put down a horse. If a horse has behavior problems, it's usually because some person caused those problems." Allie didn't like what her mother was implying. "It's not my fault Zane doesn't trust me. He dumped me. I didn't dump him. And what is so reprehensible about marrying him for his daughter's sake?"

"Allie," her mother chided gently, "I heard what you said. You married Zane to exact revenge."

"I changed my mind," Allie said defensively.

Her mother gave her a look of maternal reproach. "You're the one who says if there's a problem with a horse, a person needs to look at the problem from the horse's point of view."

Cheyenne opened the screen door and ushered her mother into the screened room with a sweeping arm gesture and a deep bow. "The Queen of Wisdom has arrived with her usual keen perception."

"Color me stupid," Allie said, "because I have no clue what you are talking about. Zane's point of view is that I'm so despicable I'd plot to make him lose his daughter."

"We'll hold off the hungry hordes," Greeley said.

Allie's sisters went into the kitchen, softly closing the screen door and the solid door behind them.

Mary sat on a battered sofa and patted the space beside her. "Why would Zane think you want him to lose Hannah?"

Allie sat with poor grace. "How should I know? I told him Hannah is his daughter. I researched the information on DNA testing for him so the matter could be settled before it became a real mess. I persuaded Sean Doyle to take the test. I did everything I could to prove to Zane that Hannah is his daughter."

"Love gets pretty complicated, doesn't it?"

"I'm not talking about love. I'm talking about trust, and the bottom line is, Zane doesn't trust me. I started the wheels in motion about the paternity tests because I thought that was best for Zane and Hannah. Why doesn't he see that?"

Mary Lassiter put an arm around Allie's shoulders and gave her a quick squeeze. "You need to be patient with Zane. Kim was unfaithful and untrustworthy. She convinced him he wasn't the father of her child. The child he'd not only accepted full responsibility for, at great personal sacrifice, but deeply loves."

"I'm not Kim Taylor."

"I know that, Allie, but look at your behavior from Zane's point of view. Greeley told me what you said at the hospital when Hannah broke her arm. She said Zane heard you. You told Zane you'd marry him, but the day of the wedding, you said you wouldn't marry him, and then you changed your mind again. How can he know what to expect from you? You admitted to him you married him for revenge. Of course he's confused and distrustful. He doesn't know what you want from him." Mary looked her middle daughter in the eye. "Do you?"

When Allie didn't answer, Mary said, "I think I'll join the others on the porch. I haven't had an opportunity to ask Kristy how she's feeling with her pregnancy."

Allie followed her mother into the house. While Mary continued down the hallway, Allie checked the beans in the oven, her mother's question echoing in her head. She didn't want anything from Zane Peters.

She certainly didn't want to be pregnant like Kristy Norton. Kristy and Jake had been trying for years to start a family. Allie had heard their hopes, their dreams.

When she and Zane had been engaged, they'd spent hours discussing the children they expected to have. How many of each sex, the names, who to pick for godparents, books they intended to read to them...

When Zane had a real wife, would he eventually want more children?

Idle curiosity prompted the question. Nothing more.

What would it be like to hold an infant version of Hannah to her breast?

She'd never know.

Favorable results of the DNA tests would change nothing. Zane was doing an excellent job of raising Hannah. Allie didn't know why he'd married her in the first place. Then the answer practically hit her in the face. Kim had convinced him he wasn't Hannah's biological father, so Zane had hoped being married would help him gain custody of Hannah if what he believed to be the truth came out.

But she was sure he was Hannah's father, so he wouldn't need Allie to stay.

Which was fine with her. She didn't want to stay.

Pinning a smile on her face, Allie went in search of Zane to ask if he was ready to cook the steaks.

He'd left the porch. Looking around she spotted him fiddling with the barbecue grill. Sean Doyle stood beside him. Not liking the tension visible between the two men, Allie hurried off the porch to join them. Deep in conversation, neither man noticed her approach.

"I'm not leaving Hannah with you." Sean said in a stubborn voice. "A jealous reporter could dig that up and twist the facts around until I looked like one of those deadbeat dads everybody fusses about. I'd lose half my female fans."

"Being Hannah's father isn't about your career," Zane said tightly. "She needs me." He paused, then added softly, "I need her."

"Look, I'm sorry, Peters, I really am. I know this mess isn't your fault, and it's too bad you got caught in the middle, but it's not like it's the end of the world for you. I can't have more kids. I had a vasectomy a couple years ago. Allie can give you all the kids you want. You won't even miss Hannah.''

Zane's face darkened with fury. ''You just proved you're not fit to be Hannah's father. Allie can't make up for losing Hannah.''

She must have made a sound because Zane abruptly turned and saw her. Sean Doyle mumbled something and walked away. He left behind a silence which stretched endlessly.

CHAPTER EIGHT

ZANE couldn't identify the emotion on Allie's face. He'd almost think she looked stricken. Which spoke volumes about his inability to read people. Allie hated him. She didn't want to bear his children. She wanted to rob him of the only child he had. He wouldn't let her. "If you'd ever had a child, you'd know they aren't replaceable like cans of peas," he said harshly.

Her face paled. "I came to tell you everything is ready. You can put the steaks on whenever you want."

Zane watched her walk away. His cruelty disgusted him. Striking out at Allie solved nothing. He knew he'd hurt her. Sorrow weighed him down. Their love, once so beautiful and full of promise, had degenerated to this ugly need to wound each other. He should call her back. To apologize. To lie to her. To tell her she'd misunderstood what he'd said to Doyle. To tell her she and her children could replace Hannah.

Resisting the urge to smash his fist into the barbecue grill, he stood silent. He'd never lied to Allie in the past, and he wasn't about to start now. Allie

and he didn't have much between them. They ought
to have the truth.

No one could replace Hannah.

With Beau Lassiter for a father, Allie couldn't
possibly understand the love a man had for his
child.

A horse whinnied in the pasture. Further away
Zane's elderly stallion answered. A younger stallion
covered the mares now, but Boreas retained a place
in Zane's heart. The black quarter horse had given
Zane and his parents years of companionship, not
to mention fathering a long line of strong-boned,
intelligent sons and daughters.

Zane wanted a son, but not to replace Hannah.
He'd love any child of his as much as he loved
Hannah. Loving one child didn't mean a man
couldn't love another. And loving Hannah as he did,
didn't mean a man couldn't love a woman.

Not that he'd ever love a woman again. He'd only
loved one woman in his life, and she'd betrayed
him.

Maybe one day he'd appreciate the irony of Allie
hating Hannah. Knowing Allie would never bear a
daughter of his, he'd named Hannah after his grandmother because Allie had loved the name. The
choice of name had been both a pathetic, sloppy,
sentimental way of keeping Allie in his heart and a
lucky talisman for Hannah. A damned curse was
more like it.

"Daddy, when we gonna get hot dogs?"

"Hot dogs!" Worth roared. "I drove all this way for hot dogs?"

Hannah's giggle constricted Zane's throat.

"Hot dogs for me and Davy, silly," she said.

"Call me silly, will you?"

Hannah dissolved into laughter as Worth swooped her up into his arms. "Silly, silly, silly!"

"He's your uncle," Greeley admonished. "You can't call him silly. You have to call him Uncle Silly."

"Uncle Silly. Uncle Silly."

Davy joined in, chanting along with Hannah. "Uncle Silly. Uncle Silly."

Davy was a good kid. He treated Hannah with a mixture of toleration and condescension, as if she were truly his younger cousin. Hannah adored the attention from Allie's family.

Hannah's maternal grandparents had refused to come to the barbecue. The only bright spot in Zane's day.

Firming his spine, Zane joined the group on the porch. He wouldn't ruin Hannah's party. For today he'd pretend life was the way he wished it were.

"I'm stuffed. Think I need to walk some of that food off." Worth hauled himself off the top step of the porch. "How 'bout you, Greeley?"

"Sure." She jumped to her feet.

"That's a good idea," Allie said, starting to rise.

"Where you going?" Worth scowled at her. "We don't want her, do we, Greeley?"

Allie's youngest sister shook her head. "We vant to be alone," she said in an exaggerated throaty voice.

Their response dumbfounded Zane. The four Lassiters were about as close as siblings could get.

He turned to Allie for enlightenment. She'd sunk back in her chair. A frown wrinkled her brow, then her eyes widened in sudden comprehension, and she became extremely interested in the porch floor.

Everyone began talking at once, in loud, stilted voices, the kind people use to get past an awkward moment. They laughed at stupid jokes, and followed with stupider jokes. Allie attempted to join in their hilarity, but Zane could tell her heart wasn't in it.

Worth and Greeley had definitely snubbed Allie. Had they heard what Allie had done and disapproved? Who the hell were they to disapprove? Zane was madder than hell at Allie siding with Doyle, but he was honest enough to admit he deserved whatever Allie threw at him.

If only she hadn't included Hannah in her revengeful plans.

"Shut your eyes," Cheyenne commanded.

Zane swung around to look at her. "What?"

"Close your eyes. You and Allie."

He looked back at Allie. She gave him a fleeting, apologetic smile, then squeezed her eyelids tight.

Zane understood neither the smile nor the embarrassed flush on her cheeks. Whatever her family had planned, Allie had guessed and she was not happy about it. She clearly expected him to be less happy. Worth and Mary Lassiter wouldn't be a party to Allie's plans for revenge, therefore whatever was going on had nothing to do with Hannah.

"Zane! Close your eyes!"

Cooperating seemed the fastest way to get answers. Zane closed his eyes. "Do you carry a whip and a chair on your tours?" he asked Cheyenne.

Thomas laughed. "You don't know the half of it. If she wasn't trying to drown me, she was trying to get me killed riding a bucking bronco. I married her in self-defense."

Everyone laughed as Cheyenne gave an unladylike snort.

"Ready?" Worth bellowed from across the yard.

A clanking and a thud followed a loud metallic rumble, and something heavy rolled toward the house.

"Okay," Worth called, "bring 'em down."

Someone took Zane's arm. "Keep your eyes closed," Cheyenne said. "Steps." She guided him across the yard. He heard Thomas guiding Allie.

"Wait for me," Hannah called.

Zane halted.

Allie ran into his back. "Oops. Sorry. I forgot she had to put on her boots."

A small hand slipped into his. "Okay," Hannah said.

He felt the tug on his hand as she skipped beside him. No one was taking his daughter from him. He'd fight for her, no matter what it took. Hannah belonged with him.

"Open your eyes," everyone chorused.

Zane blinked at the massive heap of rusty scraps of metal welded together. A huge white bow sat jauntily on top.

"For the bride and groom," Greeley said diffidently.

"Oh, Greeley," Allie said as she walked around the thing. "It's wonderful."

Zane took a second look at the twisted hunks of metal. He'd read an article in the paper about Greeley welding rusty scraps of metal together and calling it art. Allie's younger sister had been taking apart machinery and welding it back together ever since he could remember. Apparently going from fixing tractors to making stuff had been a natural step for her.

He sensed everyone waiting for him to say something. He joined Allie in walking around the heap of scrap metal while he frantically searched for an innocuous comment he could safely make. As he stared at the mass, the metal pieces seemed to take on form, and he stepped back for greater perspective. Suddenly he saw it. "It's a horse."

Everyone gave him the kind of look people reserved for idiots. He looked harder. Not one horse. Three. Two large horses and one small one. The smaller of the two large horses hovered protectively over the littlest horse. What might have been. The thought ripped painfully through Zane's mind. And caught in his throat. He plastered a big smile on his face and looked at Greeley. "I saw that article about you in the paper calling you a new talent on the art scene. This is nice.''

"Nice! It's fabulous!" Allie said. "You shouldn't have.''

The reason for the statue belatedly hit him. It was a wedding gift for him and Allie. His gaze flashed to Allie. She gave him a barely perceptible shrug of embarrassment, which told him the gift had taken her by surprise. They'd have to graciously accept and decide later what to do about the gift. "Well, thanks, Greeley.'' The overly enthusiastic thank-you sounded fake.

Allie slid her hand over the smallest horse. "It's beautiful.''

Zane wondered if anyone else heard the tiny catch in her voice. Or saw the moist shimmer in her eyes.

"A horse doesn't look like that, Daddy.''

Everyone laughed at Hannah's objection. Zane heard relief in their laughter.

"Greeley didn't copy real horses. She made what it feels like to be a horse.'' Allie took Hannah's hand and led her a few feet from the statue. "Close your eyes a little bit. Squint. Now pretend you're a little filly and you're running with your mama and your daddy. See that there?'' Allie pointed. "That's your tail flying behind you as you run.''

Hannah tipped her head one way and then the other, staring at the sculpture, her face screwed up. Suddenly her eyes widened and she said excitedly,

"I see me, I mean, I see the little filly. I like her. Is she mine?"

Greeley leaned down and kissed Hannah's cheek. "The statue is a present for all of you." Turning her head, Greeley looked directly at Zane. "Aren't you going to ask me what I call it?"

He didn't want to ask. "What?" His voice came out a croak.

"Hannah's Family." Challenge filled her voice.

Greeley must not know. Now wasn't the time to tell her. They'd find out soon enough. Doyle would probably call a press conference. If Zane thought about that now, he'd ruin Hannah's party.

He dragged his gaze from the statue and collided with a hard stare from Cheyenne. It didn't take much imagination to sense hostility from Allie's sisters. Zane wondered what Allie had told them. He glanced around the rest of the group. Allie and Hannah, joined by Davy and the Nortons, discussed the statue. Doyle stared at the statue with a puzzled expression. Steele looked sympathetically in Zane's direction while Mary gave Zane an encouraging smile. Worth winked.

What the hell was going on? Before Zane could ask, Cheyenne said, "We're next." She handed Allie a flat package wrapped in silver and white. Allie wore a fixed smile. Zane could almost see her gritting her teeth to get through this ordeal. She ripped off the paper, disclosing a large manila envelope. Her smile barely faltered as she opened it and looked inside before handing the envelope to Zane.

He pulled out glossy hotel brochures.

"For your honeymoon," Cheyenne said. "First-class suites at as many of the Steele hotels as you like, when you like, and for how long you like. Let me know, and I'll make all the arrangements. We'll keep Hannah."

Zane couldn't look at Allie. "Great."

Everyone ignored the newlyweds' obvious lack of enthusiasm.

"It's hard to top those," Kristy said, "so we didn't even try." An elaborately wrapped package magically appeared from behind Jake's back. He must have gone to their car while Zane had his eyes shut. "Zane's turn," Kristy said.

Zane took the package Jake handed him. He'd never considered wedding gifts. There had been a few when he married Kim. From relatives and her friends. Awkwardly he tugged at the bow with stiff, clumsy fingers.

"Hurry up, Daddy," Hannah urged impatiently.

"Why don't you help me?" He squatted on his haunches.

Hannah eagerly ripped the ribbon and paper from the box as Zane held it. She lifted the lid and breathed, "*Ooooh,* they're beautiful balls. Look, Daddy." She pointed. "One, two, three."

Kristy laughed. "Special balls. Hand-blown glass Christmas ones for your Christmas tree."

Pain rolled over Zane. Allie would be long gone

by Christmas. And if he lost Hannah... She could pick out her favorite and take it with her. If Doyle would let her. Allie could do what she wanted with the others. Without Allie or Hannah, Zane would never celebrate Christmas again. Or any other holiday.

"Last, but hopefully not least," Worth said in a jovial voice. He pulled a slim, narrow white packet from his shirt pocket. "From Mom and me with love."

"You open it," Zane said to Allie.

She quickly shook her head.

"I can do it," Davy said hopefully.

Everyone laughed. Cheyenne opened her mouth, but before she could explain why he couldn't, Zane handed the boy the packet. "It's your turn. Hannah opened the last."

Davy ripped off the paper. "It's a picture of a horse."

Zane's gaze flashed to Worth. Allie's brother gave him a broad grin. Slowly Zane reached for the color photograph. A well-muscled, bay quarter horse stared arrogantly at the viewer.

"Jackpot," said Worth. "Five-year-old stallion sired by Bullion. His dam is Poker Chip, who was sired by Bonanza. He's yours and Allie's. Let me know when you want him delivered."

It took all Zane's strength not to crumple the photograph. He and Worth used to talk about combining their ranches' bloodlines. They'd planned to breed one of Zane's mares to a Lassiter stallion after

Zane and Allie married. In celebration of their wedding. There had been no wedding to celebrate back then. There was still nothing to celebrate.

Thunder rumbled in the distance. A quick-moving storm had passed, more sound than fury, although rain had lashed at the windows and thunder rocked the house. Moonie had been restless, whining as he paced between bedrooms, but Hannah slept through the squall.

Despite the space of cool mattress separating them, Allie knew Zane lay awake on his side of the bed. "I told them no wedding presents." She'd made the same statement within seconds of their guests' departure. Zane hadn't answered then, and apparently had no intention of answering now.

If Allie hadn't been dumbfounded to see Sean Doyle and worried about Zane's reaction, she would have guessed what was coming as soon as she saw Worth in the pickup with Greeley and her mother as passengers and the horse trailer hitched behind.

"I should have suspected when I saw the trailer, but I thought Worth had been too lazy to unhitch it." Zane's silence spoke as eloquently as words. Worth was never too lazy.

If he'd yell at her, she could yell back. This silent condemnation got on her nerves. "Are you going to sulk forever?"

No answer.

"We won't have to stay married because of a few paltry gifts."

Zane shifted. "More than paltry."

Was there was a dollar limit that determined if a couple had to stay married? "Whatever. Greeley will have no trouble selling the sculpture. The gallery is always begging her for more. Kristy will want Hannah to have the Christmas ornaments, and we haven't actually received anything from Thomas and Cheyenne." She had to mention the final gift. Knowing about Zane's and Worth's long-ago plans, she knew what owning the stallion would mean to Zane. "There's no reason you and Worth can't work out some kind of deal with Jackpot."

"Why didn't you tell them about Hannah?"

Unable to decipher his tone of voice, Allie hesitated before saying cautiously, "I did."

"Greeley named the statue 'Hannah's Family'," he said flatly. "She wouldn't have done that if she knew Doyle was the man who got Kim pregnant."

"No, she wouldn't. She knows about Sean's claim. Cheyenne knows it, and I'm sure she told Thomas. Mom knows it. And they all agree with me that you are Hannah's father. In fact," Allie said, building up steam, "the entire Western world can see how much Hannah looks like you, except for four blind, very stupid people. You, Sean and the Taylors."

Turning his back to her, Zane pretended to sleep. Allie wasn't fooled. She wished the darned test results would get here. So she could leave. Get on with the rest of her life. Possibilities abounded. She loathed them all.

Neither of them slept a wink. Allie could almost hear Zane greet the dawn with a sigh of relief as he practically leaped out of bed and grabbed his clothes.

He didn't bother being quiet. So he knew she lay awake.

Allie made herself stay in bed. Giving him time to eat and escape the house.

The front door closed. Throwing back the covers, she left the bed and stole over to the window. Zane stood in front of the metal sculpture, so still he might have been a statue himself.

Hannah loved the sculpture. She wouldn't understand why it had to go away. Maybe Greeley could cut the statue apart. Remove the mare. Weld the two remaining horses back together. Father and daughter. A closed unit.

Ruth or Allie had picked up the mail and dropped it on his desk. Slumped in his chair, Zane had no idea how long he'd been staring at the unopened envelope on top of the stack. He couldn't make himself reach for it.

The sounds of a horse trotting came through the open office window. Allie must be putting the paint through her paces.

He got up and headed outdoors. If he stayed in the office another second, his whole body would explode through his skin. The envelope could wait.

Until now he'd made a point of being elsewhere when Allie worked with the filly so she couldn't

accuse him of checking on her. He hoped she'd take
offense at his appearance. A furious, no-holds-
barred argument might take his mind off the envelope. Pain ripped his insides. An out-of-control, ten-
ton truck speeding toward him couldn't take his
mind off the envelope.

Copper stood outside the round pen, her reins
loosely tied to a post. Hannah sat in Allie's saddle
on the large mare, her attention riveted to the action
in the pen.

Allie flapped a saddle blanket on and around the
filly. The paint watched, her eyes interested. Zane
could hardly believe she was the same wild-eyed
horse he'd trailered home kicking and screaming.
The filly's ears flicked in his direction, but she
didn't move.

Allie looked over at him. "She's going to be a
sweetheart, Zane. She's eager to please and smart."

Hannah turned her head. "Daddy, look! I'm riding Copper."

"I see." Hannah had been riding his gentlest
horse for over a year. Zane knew Allie's elderly
horse from the many hours he used to spend on the
Lassiter ranch, and while Copper might be large, the
mare was as reliable as a favorite nanny.

Resting his arm on the mare's hindquarters, Zane
clutched the back of the mare's saddle. Once he
opened that envelope, it would be official. He
wouldn't be entitled to call Hannah his daughter.
The loving, the caring, the raising—they'd count for

nothing. Nothing would count but biology. The hell with that!

Allie watched Zane out of the corner of her eye as she worked with the filly. His hat shaded his eyes, but she could see the taut lines drawn around his mouth, and the rigid set to his jaw. The way he held his body as if warding off blows. Something terrible had happened.

The filly gave her a curious look, sensing Allie's tension. Another time Allie might have smiled at the horse's discernment. The filly was too young for Hannah now, but as they matured, they'd make wonderful companions. She thought once again that Zane had always had a good eye for picking a horse.

Zane. She couldn't work with the horse with her attention centered on Zane. Every cell in her body screamed to know what was wrong.

Allie opened the gate and the filly trotted into the pasture. After a few yards, the paint turned and blew air through her nose in Allie's direction, then wheeled and cantered toward the small herd on the far side of the pasture. The filly had started the little ritual about a week ago. It reminded Allie how her students used to call goodbye to her as they climbed in the school bus. "Goodbye," she called to the paint. "See you tomorrow."

"Was Honey good today?" Hannah asked anxiously.

Allie let herself out of the pen. "Very good. She knew you were watching."

"I touched her, Daddy," Hannah said proudly. "Me and Allie rode Copper by Honey and I petted her. She liked it."

Allie frowned as she saw Zane's white-knuckled grip on the saddle. "I wouldn't let Hannah do anything I didn't think perfectly safe."

Zane gave her a blank look. "What?"

Obviously this wasn't about Hannah riding Copper or touching Honey. Allie lifted Hannah down from the mare. "Go wash up. I'll be in as soon as I take care of Copper."

"Don't wanna go in and wash."

"Ruth made spaghetti. After you wash your hands thoroughly, you may put some of those pretty paper napkins on the table."

Hannah ran toward the house.

Allie undid Copper's reins and looked at Zane. Seeing the bleak glaze in his eyes, she reached over and touched his hand glued to her saddle. "I want to put Copper with the other horses," she said gently. "You need to let go of her."

He stared at Allie, then at his hand. Abruptly he released his grip on the saddle and jammed his hands into his pockets as he stared down at the ground.

Unbuckling Copper's saddle, Allie flung it and the mare's saddle blanket over the top rung of the pen before she turned Copper loose in the pasture.

Zane slugged a fence post.

Allie's heart literally stopped. She'd brought in the mail. She'd seen the envelope. Zane's reaction could mean only one thing. She had trouble breathing. No. It couldn't be right. She wasn't wrong. Not about this. "We'll do the tests again," she said quickly. "Somewhere else. They're wrong. They made a mistake. They had to have."

"I don't remember much about sleeping with Kim that night. I'd had more than a few drinks and the next thing I remember is waking up naked beside Kim in her bed. I had one hell of a headache. It was all a blur to me. Guess I didn't want to remember the details. Later, she laughed about that night. Said she was looking for a sucker because Doyle wouldn't marry her even though she was pregnant with his child. She said I never touched her, that I'd passed out before I could."

"You touched her. Hannah's proof of that. I don't care what Kim said. Or what that stupid company's stupid test said."

"Cut it out, Allie. I could lose Hannah. Isn't that revenge enough for you? Does teasing me with false hope increase your pleasure or some damn sick thing like that?"

"It's not false hope. You are Hannah's father. Physical evidence doesn't lie. Okay, so DNA is physical, but they messed up the test. Accidentally switched the names or something. We'll do it again. And if we get the same stupid answer, we'll do something else. I don't care what you say. The courts won't take Hannah away from you."

He didn't look at her, just shook his head.

"What exactly did the letter say?" She may as

well have asked her question of the fence post. Whirling around, Allie whipped across the yard and into the house.

The envelope sat on Zane's desk.

Unopened. The idiot!

Snatching the envelope from the desk, Allie ripped it open. If Zane didn't like her opening his mail, that was too darned bad. Taking only a second to read the contents, she stormed back outside to the corral. Zane hadn't moved.

Allie thrust the information in his face. "Read this."

Pushing her hand aside, he said tonelessly, "I don't need to. I know what it says."

"When did you develop the ability to read through sealed envelopes?"

"Go away, Allie. You've had your fun."

"Fun?" Allie yelled. "My fun hasn't even begun. First I'm going to kick you in the behind because you're so darned stupid and stubborn. That'll be fun. In fact, it will be so much fun, I think I'll kick you more than once. Maybe I'll hog-tie you and throw you on the ground and jump up and down on your entire backside until you scream for mercy. That will really be fun. And when Hannah comes out to see what's going on, I'll tell her I'm having fun trying to kick some sense into her stupid, stubborn mule of a father."

"Let it go. I—" He spun around. "What did you say?"

"I said stupid, stubborn mule."

"You said, 'her father.' Give me that."

"Why? You already know what it says. Remember?"

"Allie," he said in a warning voice.

"Zane," she mimicked, holding the letter behind her and backing away. "You told me to go away. I'm going." Turning, she ran for the house. She deserved her pound of flesh after the way Zane had scared the living daylights out of her. Leading her to believe the DNA test proved he wasn't Hannah's father when he hadn't even opened the darned envelope. If he wasn't bigger than her, she'd turn around and slug him. Well, the heck with that. Skidding to a stop, Allie whirled around and threw a punch.

Dodging her swing, Zane gave her a disgusted look and hauled her against his hard body, in the process grabbing the paper.

Allie tried to squirm away from the hammerlock grip around her waist. "I'm going to make you sorry."

"Go ahead," he said absently, his gaze devouring the piece of paper.

She relaxed against him. A person couldn't have a decent fight with another person until she had his complete attention.

"I'm Hannah's father," Zane said softly, his voice filled with stunned disbelief. "I really am her father. Kim was lying when she said I wasn't Hannah's father. I am her father."

Allie blinked moisture from her eyes. "I told you so." Trying to sound smug, she failed utterly.

"Hannah's my daughter." He laughed. "She's been my daughter all along." Releasing Allie, Zane took off his hat and tossed it high in the air. "My daughter!" he yelled at the top of his lungs. Dancing like a maniac across the yard, he kept yelling, "Mine, mine, mine!" Blindly colliding with the corral, Zane turned his back to Allie and wrapped his hands around the nearest post. His shoulders shook silently.

Once Allie would have gone to him, thrown her arms around him, shared his overwhelming relief. Once was long ago. Then she and Zane had shared their thoughts, their joys, their sorrows. Their lives. Their futures. Now they shared only a bed.

The sun rolled over the western horizon sending orange streaks high into the sky where they pierced charcoal-colored clouds. The air felt heavy and oppressive. In the pasture, the horses nervously faced into the wind.

Near her foot a patch of dandelions had gone to seed. Allie ground a puffball under her foot and went into the house.

A bolt of lightning flashed to the northwest, followed by the dull mutter of thunder. Standing at the open bedroom window, Allie smelled ozone in the air.

"We might get some more rain."

Her back to the door, she hadn't heard Zane enter

the room. "Yes." Allie felt the awkwardness of their marriage more tonight than at any time since their hasty wedding. Her earlier reluctance to intrude on Zane's private moment at the corral emphasized the chasm between them. She would have hugged a friend. Or even a stranger.

She should have been able to rejoice with Zane. His good news was hers. Proof that Hannah was his biological daughter gave Allie her ticket to freedom.

Their ill-conceived marriage was over. Zane could be consigned to her past where he belonged. All ties, all strings, all connection between them, severed.

Whatever had been between them was finally dead.

Zane moved to stand beside her. "I thought I'd explode at dinner not talking about it."

"I know." He hadn't been able to take his eyes off Hannah, laughing too loud at her childish silliness. When she'd accidentally spilled her milk, he'd kissed her nose and told her he loved her.

"I put off telling Hannah, and there's no point saying anything now," he said. "It's not something a four-year-old could understand. Maybe when she gets older, I don't know. I'd have to tell her about Kim, and I'd rather not say negative things about her mother. Then again, she could hear something from somebody else. Maybe I should say something."

"You don't have to decide now." Allie's hands

felt heavy. She couldn't lift them from the windowsill.

"Doyle phoned. He said he and Kim had an affair for several months while he was in Aspen filming a ski movie. That was before his TV success, and he only had a minor role and couldn't afford to bring his family. He'd used protection when he slept with Kim but assumed it had failed. He never knew Kim slept with me before we married, so he was positive Hannah was his because of the timing."

"I suspect Kim didn't know who Hannah's father was," Allie said hesitantly. "If she slept with you while sleeping with Sean... So she wasn't really lying."

Zane grunted. "When Doyle refused to leave his wife to marry Kim and broke off the affair, Kim latched onto me to support her. Poor Kim. Trying to steal what she wanted, she ended up with nothing, but she gave me Hannah."

Allie would never give him a child.

"Doyle will never be the man he could be if he sidesteps all his obligations. I feel sorry for him. He really does miss his family."

After excruciating days of imagining the worst, Zane would identify with the man's pain. Allie's sympathy lay elsewhere. "I feel sorry for his boys. If their parents are fighting for custody, the children will be the ones to suffer the most. At least Mom and Beau never put us through that."

Zane lightly touched her shoulder, then dropped

his hand. "Thanks to you, Hannah won't have to suffer."

"The truth would have come out sooner or later."

"You were so sure."

Allie would never admit how scared she'd been that she might be wrong. "Anyone looking at Hannah can see the Peters in her."

"I called my parents tonight to tell them the test results. My mother had thought on it all week, and she vaguely recalls hearing her grandfather's mother had red curly hair. The only picture I've seen of the woman was in black and white."

Being proven right didn't bring the satisfaction it should have. A vague depression hovered below the surface of Allie's consciousness. She probed it, as one probed for the source of an aching tooth.

She felt happy for Zane and Hannah. She shared Zane's joy.

Except she didn't. She shared nothing.

Zane hadn't shared his joy.

He hadn't shared his vulnerability.

He'd turned his back to Allie, shutting her out.

A bolt of lightning streaked through the sky. Out of habit, Allie counted the seconds before a loud clap of thunder sounded. The storm had moved closer. Feeling chilled, she wrapped her arms around herself, rubbing her arms with her hands.

Lightning flashed again, the bright jagged lines etching themselves on her eyeballs as she faced what she'd been trying to ignore since Zane read the DNA report. Zane didn't need her. Not when he had Hannah.

Sleep wouldn't come. Zane folded an arm over his eyes. As if blocking his sight prevented him from seeing what a fool he'd been. He'd made a mess of everything. No wonder Allie had walked away when he'd lost control at the corral.

He used to pride himself on being fearless and brave. That pride lay discarded in the dust. From the moment Kim first told him he wasn't Hannah's father, he'd lived with the gut-wrenching fear he'd lose his daughter.

He'd taken his fear out on Allie. Accused her of betraying him. Of plotting against him. He had even tried to convince himself he'd stopped loving Allie. That he hated her.

Yet on some level, he'd known he hadn't stopped loving her. Nothing else explained the way he needed her. The way he ached to make love to her. With his last breath he'd love her.

He lacked the guts to tell her so. How could he after betraying her five years ago? After doubting her last week. After the accusations he'd flung at her. Love meant trust, loyalty, commitment. Not angry words, doubt and betrayal.

They hadn't spoken since coming to bed. Zane hadn't known what to say. Hadn't known how to apologize. Searching for the right words, he'd said nothing, and the silence between them had deepened and thickened until it became an impenetrable barrier. Allie would have fallen asleep hours ago.

She'd have nothing but contempt if he offered her his worthless love.

Zane couldn't bear losing her a second time.

His fists tightened. A man couldn't lose what he didn't have.

"You shouldn't have any more trouble with the Taylors over custody. Even they have to realize no judge would grant them custody after what they tried to pull," Allie said quietly.

"I thought you were asleep."

"No." A heartbeat later, she said, "I'll leave in the morning."

He couldn't let her go and scrambled for a compelling reason to persuade her to stay. "Custody is probably no longer an issue, but Edie is right about Hannah needing a mother." Taking a deep breath, Zane risked it all. "We agreed to give our marriage a month's trial run to see if we could manage a workable relationship."

"That was before you told me to pack up and leave and said it was too late to try to make our marriage work."

"I was wrong and I apologize."

She said nothing.

"I was scared, okay?" he asked belligerently. "I'd come up against something I didn't know how to fight, and in my fear, I struck out at you. It's not an excuse. It's a reason and a rotten one, but it's the truth. Damn it, I'm sorry." As an apology, it stunk. No wonder Allie didn't rush to accept it.

After a bit she asked, "You want me to stay for Hannah's sake? Or because you feel guilty about accusing me of horrible things? Or out of gratitude?"

"For Hannah's sake." That answer would do for now. He didn't dare tell her he wanted her in his bed, at his dinner table, riding his horses, sharing his life. He'd thrown away the right to say any of that.

"The sex is good," she said unexpectedly. "Isn't it?"

own fault. When she left, she would break he had of her. Memories of her in his bed. He should have made love to her tonight.

She gave a small, quiet laugh. "We were certainly young and dumb. We actually believed in romance and ..."

Her comment danced here, but now wasn't as ...

CHAPTER NINE

ALLIE'S comment surprised a choke of laughter from Zane. "Very good." His amusement vanished. He hadn't made love to her tonight. Remorse had held him back. He'd wanted to love her. Wanted her arms holding him. Wanted himself buried in her. To thank her. To apologize. To make himself whole.

He needed her.

"Once we thought we loved each other. Wait," she said at the sound of protest he made. "Let me finish. We were in love, but that wasn't enough to keep our relationship from disintegrating."

"What happened had nothing to do with our loving each other," Zane said quickly, turning toward her. "It had to do with how stupid I was." He watched her chest rise and fall with each breath she took.

"The point is, all that can't-live-without-you-heart-pounding turned out to be insubstantial fluff. It would never have supported a marriage...it didn't even support an engagement."

"We're different people now. Older, and hopefully wiser." He tried to memorize her face in the dim light. When she left, this would be all he had of her. Memories of her in his bed. He should have made love to her tonight.

She gave a small, rueful laugh. "We were certainly young and unwise. We actually believed in happily ever after."

Her cynicism dismayed him, but now wasn't the time to try to argue her out of it. "We have a lot in common, families, backgrounds. We both grew up on ranches. In spite of what happened, I think we have the same values. We used to like and respect each other. If we work at it, I believe we can, not forget the past, but put it in the past. I think we can work together on a common goal."

"Raising Hannah?"

"Marriage. A real marriage. You committed to a month. Would it be so bad to stay at least that long and try?"

"I'm not sure our getting married was the best thing for Hannah. She's already lost her mother. What happens when I leave?"

Not if. When. He steeled himself with the knowledge that he had the rest of the month to change "when" into never. If he could convince her to stay that long. "You could still see each other. Even if you and I can't work things out, we ought to be able to part amicably. Hannah could visit you in Aspen or at the Double Nickel."

"Do you honestly think it's possible for us to have a friendly, platonic relationship?"

Her troubled voice told him she was considering

it. He wouldn't allow himself to hope. Not yet. One could never assume with Allie. "No."

She swallowed, her throat muscles working hard. "That's honest, anyway. You're right, of course." She swallowed again. "With our past, there's no way we could be friends."

The workings of her throat muscles fascinated him. Allie sounded almost disappointed. Raising himself up on an elbow, he said, "I don't know if we can be friends." Zane lightly touched the base of her throat. "But I know we sure as hell can't have a platonic relationship."

His body tightened at her racing pulse. Only Allie could turn him on with something as ordinary as blood pumping through her veins. Briefly he touched the sexy, pulsing spot with his lips, then lifting his head, he slowly smiled into her eyes. "As you said, the sex is very good."

Her mouth was moist and tasted minty from toothpaste. He told himself to slow down. He couldn't slow down. She wouldn't let him. He lifted his head, to breathe. To look at her.

"I said good. I didn't say very good," she murmured.

Zane laughed, breathing in her unique scent, which brought to mind summer wildflowers and exotic spices and tousled sheets. "I suppose—" he undid the top button of her pajama top "—that's a challenge to me—" he moved to the second button "—to change good—" he worked loose the next button "—into very good." He unbuttoned the last button.

"I suppose—" her breath caught as he slowly slid the cool, slick fabric over her breasts "—you could look at it that way."

Zane curved his thumbs around the tips of her breasts, unbelievably aroused by their instant hardening. Giving in to a compelling need to stroke smooth, silky skin, he said, "I believe in rising to a challenge."

Warm hands slid beneath the waistband of his undershorts. Shifting beneath him, Allie laughed softly. "I noticed."

Zane kissed the laughter from her willing mouth as mingled triumph and desire surged through him. Allie Lassiter in his bed for the touching. The kissing. The loving. Her bare body warming him. Her long legs tangled with his. The two of them joining in the most basic, intimate way. Everything he'd ever wanted.

With one exception.

She no longer loved him. If she ever had.

He didn't know if he could live with an Allie who didn't love him.

The hell of it was, he knew for damned sure he couldn't live without her.

She couldn't believe she'd agreed to stay until the month was up.

Hannah didn't need her. Neither did Zane. Why had he asked her to stay? Delicious memories sent pleasurable aftershocks to her midsection. Maybe he wanted a woman in his bed. Any woman.

Allie immediately discarded that explanation. A man like Zane could have his pick of women.

Kim Taylor had been a fool. With a husband, a lover, like Zane, why in the world had Kim taken other lovers? Granted, Kim and Zane's relationship had not been based on mutual love, but then neither was Allie and Zane's. Allie smiled. She certainly had no complaints.

"Why the silly grin?"

Allie looked across the car at Cheyenne. "Why not? It's a beautiful September day. The sky is blue, the aspen are turning gold, sunflowers and wild asters are blooming everywhere."

"And Zane has received back the DNA results and knows the truth."

"That, too."

Cheyenne glanced into the back seat of Allie's car where Davy and Hannah played with Davy's toy cars before asking, "Did you make him grovel for accusing you of plotting against him?"

"He apologized. He was upset."

"You mean he gave a bunch of stupid excuses for acting like a jerk."

"He did feel bad," Allie said.

"If you're defending him, I guess there's hope."

Allie turned onto a rutted ranch road and stopped. "You can get the gate."

Cheyenne hopped out.

The gate had come at an opportune time. Allie

had no intention of discussing her marriage with her older sister. Thomas thought the moon rose and set on Cheyenne. Once Zane had looked that way at Allie. She drove slowly through the opened gate, and waited for Cheyenne.

Back in Allie's vehicle, Cheyenne looked in the back seat again and said quietly, "I don't think Thomas will ever quit regretting the estrangement with his brother. Or quit blaming himself. David's death took away any option of Thomas and David reconciling. It's the saddest thing in the world. Thomas will never have another brother."

Allie heaved a loud sigh. "Okay, Cheyenne. What's the message? Spit it out."

Cheyenne grimaced. "Thomas says I'm about as subtle as a sledgehammer."

Envy clawed at Allie. Her sister said her husband's name in such a loving voice. Thomas didn't love Cheyenne because she was perfect. He loved her because she was Cheyenne. What would it be like to love and be loved like that? Allie shoved aside her envy. "Sledgehammers are much subtler. What is it you're trying to tell me?"

"We can't throw away the important things in life because of stupid things like pride." Cheyenne hesitated. "Or revenge."

Allie brought the car to a stop. The mares in the pasture stared at the vehicle while their foals stood at their mothers' sides, curiosity writ on their long faces. "Here we are," Allie said. "Davy, if we walk toward them slowly, the foals will probably

come right up to us.'' Like Worth, Zane started
working with his foals at birth, and they'd have no
fear of humans. The mares, trusting, but alert for
trouble, watched the humans. A tiny bay colt
pranced toward them.

"He's adorable,'' Cheyenne said.

"That's Mosquito. Daddy said he's everywhere.
His mama is Imogene. Hi, Imogene,'' Hannah
called to the large standard bay. The mare placidly
moved in their direction.

Davy ducked behind Cheyenne. "She's big.''

Reaching them, the mare nickered gently. Allie
rubbed the bay mare's neck. "Go ahead and rub
Mosquito's neck the way I'm rubbing his mama's.''

Cheyenne showed Davy how, then she worked
with the colt's head. "Zane's done a good job. This
little fellow doesn't mind being touched anywhere.''

"Here comes Tar-something.'' Hannah wrinkled
her face. "I can't remember. Daddy said it's a
bird.''

"Ptarmigan,'' Allie guessed.

Busy petting the small filly, Hannah didn't answer.

"Does she know all their names?'' Cheyenne
asked quietly.

"Zane takes her with him whenever he can.''
Allie flashed back to Zane saying he'd been in the
delivery room. She visualized him holding Hannah
seconds after her birth, talking to her, patting her,
bonding with her.

"Hard to remember he's the same man who be-

lieved in partying hard,'' Cheyenne said. ''When he
did some rodeoing in college, I thought he'd take it
up, but then Buck and Dolly moved to Texas, and
Zane took over this place. Settled him down.''

Allie shook her head. ''Hannah settled him down.
He knows if he shirks his responsibilities, she could
suffer.

''Making him more than he was, instead of less.
Maybe you ought to think about that.''

Allie had thought about it. A lot. Zane had matured, grown into his potential, become a man a person could rely on. She wondered now if Zane had
been as reckless as she feared five years ago, or if
her own fears and insecurities, brought about by
having Beau as a father, had led her to imagine
weakness where none existed. No doubt the truth
lay somewhere in between.

Allie sat in a chair on the front porch, her feet
propped on the porch railing. The metal porch glider
creaked as Zane pushed it back and forth. The sun
had disappeared over the Elk Mountains, but the
earth held on to its heat for a little while longer.
Soon they'd have to put on coats or go inside.

''We saw the foals today. Davy was scared of the
mares.'' Hannah propped her feet on one end of the
glider, in imitation of Allie. Her head rested in her
father's lap.

Zane wrapped a red tendril around his finger.
''When Grandpa Buck took you to the rodeo, you
didn't like the clowns.''

"I didn't know they was Grandpa's friends. I never saw clowns before."

"Davy hasn't been around horses much. He lived in a big city where there are cars and buses and subways but not many horses."

"What's a subway?"

"A train that goes underground."

Hannah's eyes widened. "Like prairie dogs?"

As Zane explained, Allie's mind drifted to her earlier conversation with Cheyenne. Allie knew what her sister meant. Allie couldn't turn back the clock. Five years ago the door had closed on the future she'd dreamed of. That future didn't happen, couldn't happen, never would happen.

Allie couldn't pretend those years hadn't happened. Kim Taylor had died, but Allie couldn't pretend Zane hadn't married her. The way Allie had been pretending. Calling the woman Kim Taylor. She'd been Kim Peters. Zane's first wife. He'd slept with her, made love to her, been there when she gave birth to his—their—daughter. Those were the facts. They would always be the facts.

Allie had no choice when Zane broke their engagement. She had a choice now. She could walk away. Tonight, tomorrow, at the end of the month, whenever she wanted. Or she could stay married to Zane. Commit to building a future with him. Not the future she'd once planned, but a different future.

"Allie!"

Zane's tone told her he'd been calling her name for some time. "What?"

"Hannah asked you something."

Allie smiled at the little girl.

"How come you don't sit with us?"

"You two are too big. There's no room."

"Yes, there is. You can hold my feet."

"As if I'd want to hold two stinky feet."

Hannah sat up and scooted around. "Daddy will."

"Well, if your daddy likes stinky feet." Allie sat at the other end of the glider.

Hannah put her head in Allie's lap and lifted her feet. "You like my stinky feet, don't you, Daddy?"

Zane captured her feet in one large hand and held them to his nose. "I love your stinky feet." He inhaled deeply. "They smell like Allie's neck." He laid his hand along the back of the glider. His fingers brushed the top of Allie's spine.

Hannah giggled. "Allie has a stinky neck." She rested her feet on Zane's shoulder. "Allie put her smelly stuff in my bathwater and I had lots of bubbles."

Zane smiled at Allie over Hannah. "That was nice of Allie."

"I'm a nice person."

His fingers toyed with her neck. "Very nice."

Nice didn't seem such a disparaging word when a heavy-lidded, sensuous look accompanied it. Allie felt heat coiling deep within her. Waiting. Anticipating. Darn him. A man shouldn't look so darned sexy when he sat on a glider with his daughter's bare feet resting on him. He had no business giving a woman a "come to bed" look when he knew darned well they were hours from bed.

Two could play his game. Looking away, Allie smiled demurely and trailed her hand down Hannah's side to rest it on Zane's thigh. Fingers tightened around her neck. Her gaze flashed triumphantly to his, then her breath caught. Naked desire darkened Zane's eyes to midnight-blue. Allie wanted to launch herself into the depths of those smoldering eyes.

"Daddy! Daddy!" Hannah pushed a heel against Zane. "Tell me a story 'bout the girl."

Zane stilled, then looking away from Allie, suggested in an offhand voice, "How about the story about the mama bear who brought her babies to visit? I'll bet Allie doesn't know it."

"I wanna hear 'bout the girl. Tell the one 'bout her being a mama to baby birds and feeding them bugs. Allie don't know that story."

To the contrary. Allie knew that story very well. She stared at Zane in astonishment.

He avoided looking at her. "There was this girl—"

"Jane Donut," Hannah prompted.

"Jane Donut. One day Jane was walking home from the school bus—"

"With her bruther and two sisters."

"Who's telling this story, you or me?"

Hannah giggled. "You, Daddy."

"Okay. Jane's walking and she found—"

"Baby birds. Their mama and daddy was playing

with angels." Hannah clapped her hands over her mouth.

Giving her a playfully fierce look, Zane continued, lavishly embellishing his story with fanciful twists and turns. Allie wouldn't have recognized the plucky heroine if she walked past her on the street. Which was odd since Allie had been the girl rescuing the bluebirds after a stray cat had eaten the parents.

Hannah sighed gustily at the happy conclusion. "Daddy knows lots of stories about Jane Donut. She helped animals all the time 'cuz she loved animals, right, Daddy?"

"She still does, honey."

"How come you know her, Daddy?"

"I loved her."

"Me, too," Hannah said firmly. "We both love her, don't we, Daddy?"

Zane hadn't answered Hannah's question. He didn't have to. Sitting at breakfast the next morning, Allie knew the answer. He'd used love in the past tense.

Love. How she hated that word. What did it mean? Did it mean melting inside when a man smiled at you in a certain way? Was it knocking knees when a man undressed in front of you? Or incredible sensations when you made love to him?

Or was it the quiet contentment a person felt when a man listened to his daughter's prayers? The admiration for the way he was raising his child with gentleness and loving discipline?

Allie had always known Zane's good qualities.
The way he treated animals. And people. Cowboys
were too independent to stick with an unfair boss,
and most of his hands had worked for him forever.
Zane practiced wise stewardship of the land.

She twisted the wedding band on her finger.

"You never asked me about that," Zane said,
watching her.

She knew it was his great-grandmother's ring.
He'd planned to put it on Allie's finger five years
ago. When he produced it the morning of their wedding, she'd objected, unable to stomach wearing a
ring Kim had worn. Obviously guessing her reasons
for objecting, Zane had told her Kim never wore
this ring.

"You didn't ask why I bought a different ring for
Kim."

"I assumed she wanted something more mod-
ern."

"She never saw this ring. I couldn't give it to
her. Not when it was supposed to be your ring."

Not knowing how to respond, Allie held out her
hand. "I've always liked it."

"You can keep it. No matter what happens." He
shoved back his chair. "Thanks for fixing me breakfast."

"You're welcome." She wasn't sure why she'd
risen early and cooked him bacon and eggs.

He stood across the table, his hands on the back
of his chair. "We're stacking hay today. I don't

know when I'll be home. If I'm late, don't wait dinner for me.''

"All right." They sounded like any long-married couple.

"Well—" his fingers tapped the chair "—have a good day."

"You, too."

Zane didn't leave, but stood there, looking at her.

She'd combed her hair in a hurry. It must be a mess. Allie ran a hand over it. Her imagination filled the silence between them with unspoken words with hidden meanings. Blindly she groped for her coffee mug, but a strange paralysis kept her from raising the mug from the table.

He had a strong face. A rugged jaw. An adorable cleft to his chin. A woman could warm herself in the depths of dark, velvety blue eyes.

He'd warmed her beautifully last night.

She wanted him to kiss her. Heat rose to her cheeks and she dropped her gaze before Zane read her thoughts.

He walked around the table. "That was the best breakfast I've ever had."

She couldn't help laughing as his words pointed out the divergent paths their thoughts had taken. Not to mention the absurdity of the remark. "I'll have to remember you like your bacon burned."

Zane pulled her to her feet. "Remember more than that." He crushed her lips beneath his.

Who knew the taste of bacon and coffee could be so exciting? Allie clung to him, weaving her fingers through his hair. Her feet bumped into his boots and she curled her bare toes over the scarred leather tops. Zane's hands gripped her hips through her robe and pajamas as he thoroughly explored the depths of her mouth. With each beat of his heart, the scent of soap from his morning shower eddied in the air along with his personal, masculine scent.

When he slowly removed his mouth from hers, Allie shared his reluctance.

"Damned hay," he muttered. "If I don't get down to the barn, Wally's going to come up here looking for me." Shimmering desire evolved into wry amusement. "He'd probably be a little surprised if he found us making love on the kitchen table."

"Not to mention what Ruth would think if she came in."

Zane gave Allie a lopsided smile. "It would be your fault for looking so damned sexy in the morning." He ran his finger down her cheek. "I love this little wrinkle your pillow made."

"You silver-tongued devil." Allie laughingly pushed away his hand. "Go to work." As he walked out of the kitchen, she remembered the fanciful story he'd told Hannah and called after him, "I don't remember any dinosaur or a handsome prince slaying bird-eating dragons when I took those baby bluebirds home."

"I'm sure there was a handsome prince," came his laughing reply.

Ruth walked into the kitchen. "You must be talking about Zane's Jane Donut stories. There's a handsome prince in all of them,'' the older woman said, eyeing the skillet askance.

"I'll wash it," Allie said quickly.

"I'm a pro at burned pans. I've had lots of practice."

"Thanks." Allie dropped a quick kiss on Ruth's cheek. "Then I'll take a shower before Hannah gets up." She stopped in the kitchen doorway. "A handsome prince in all of them?"

"I guess he figured if he couldn't get the girl in real life, he could get her in his stories." Ruth shook her head. "The things you got up to. I'd forgotten half of them."

Allie fled to the shower. With water cascading around her, she leaned against the cool tile, a silly look on her face, and thanked whatever shred of common sense had kept her from sweeping the dishes from the table and making love with Zane.

Making love. However Zane had meant the words, Allie knew exactly what she meant when she thought them.

Making love. Not having sex.

So busy hating the Zane who'd jilted her, Allie didn't know when she'd started loving the man Zane had become. Cheyenne had put her finger on the essential truth. Allie could fill her life with bitterness and revenge. Or she could close the door on the past and accept the golden possibilities before her.

Zane would never be a saint. He had flaws. As if

she didn't. None of that mattered. What mattered
was Allie loved him. He'd drive her crazy at times,
annoy her. They'd fight. How they'd fight. They'd
also make up. Allie idly ran the soapy washcloth
over her breasts. She looked forward to making up.

She'd have to thank Cheyenne. Horrible thought.
Allie might as well give her older sister an engraved
invitation to interfere. Allie turned her grinning face
up to the spray of water. Cheyenne deserved her
triumph.

The past would be relegated to the past. Who
cared about the past when the future held such
promise? Allie no longer naively believed marriage
to Zane meant a perfect life. There would be rough
spots, hard times, struggles, but Zane would be at
her side to share them. She'd be at his side.

He didn't love her. Allie considered that. She
hadn't exactly been lovable. She loved him. She
loved Hannah. Surely that was enough to start with.

Her mind made up, she squirted shampoo on her
hair. Zane had insisted on marrying her, and he'd
have to live with the consequences whether he loved
Allie or not. He was going to have to learn to love
his wife. His wife. For better or worse.

Even if they hadn't said the words.

Small knuckles rapped on the shower door. "Allie?"

Allie saw Hannah's rippled silhouette through the
shower stall's glass door. Zane's wife meant
Hannah's mother.

Wearing a goofy grin, Allie reached for her towel

and stepped out of the shower. Her sleepy-eyed daughter smiled back.

Ruth looked up from the kitchen sink as the screen door to the back porch slammed shut behind Zane. "You're early."

"Moving and stacking the hay bales went quicker than expected, so I told your husband to call it an early day. You might as well take off, and go home and hold hands with him."

The housekeeper snorted. "Wally'll have a beer in one hand and the TV remote in the other. We're not newlyweds like some people I know."

Zane laughed. He'd never been able to fool Ruth. Working for his parents, she'd helped raise him. Kim had wanted to fire Ruth, but Zane refused, and Kim quickly came to appreciate the benefits of having Ruth around to cook, do the housework and care for Hannah. Ruth and Zane had never discussed Zane's first wife, and they never would.

Just as they'd never discussed Allie. Ruth had always liked Allie, but not by so much as a single word or action had she shown her disappointment when Zane messed up and had to marry Kim. Ruth had treated Kim like a guest. She treated Allie like a friend. Speaking of Allie... "Where's my family?" He loved saying that. His family.

"Allie went to Aspen and took Hannah with her."

For no logical reason, an uneasy feeling crawled

up Zane's spine. "She took Hannah? Just like that?"

"Isn't that okay?"

"Sure, it's okay." Allie had acted oddly this morning. Cooking his breakfast. He should have questioned why. There'd been tension in the air. He'd labeled it sexual. Now he wondered. "I just thought, well, Allie didn't mention going anywhere."

"She didn't decide to go until after Hannah ate breakfast. She called for an appointment to get her hair cut, and the salon had a cancellation this afternoon. With you eating lunch in the field, Allie thought Hannah might enjoy going along."

He couldn't dismiss his vague apprehension. "You know I don't like Hannah riding in a car without her child safety seat."

"Allie took the seat from my car." Removing her apron, Ruth hung it on a hook. "They should be back soon. There's a pot roast in the oven." She paused with her hand on the doorknob. "Allie won't let anything happen to Hannah. She knows how to deal with the likes of the Taylors. You don't need to worry."

"You're right." Zane managed a smile. "I'm sure everything's fine. They'll be home before I get out of the shower."

Hannah was perfectly safe with Allie, Zane told himself as he stepped into the shower stall. Allie taking Hannah to Aspen was no different from Ruth taking Hannah to the grocery store. He'd never worried about Hannah when she went with Ruth.

Ruth had never sat at the breakfast table measuring him with her eyes. Never tried to butter him up by doing something unexpected, something nice for him. As Kim did when she wanted something from Zane. He'd learned that the nicer Kim was, the less he could trust her.

He hadn't a clue what Allie had been thinking this morning.

Which wasn't a reason to worry. A man could go crazy trying to figure out what a woman was thinking. He wasn't worried. He was... Zane thought about it a minute. Annoyed, he decided. He was annoyed.

Common courtesy dictated Allie check with him before cavalierly walking off with his daughter. What if he'd had plans to do something with Hannah this afternoon? Take her for a ride or something. Zane lathered his body with increasing irritation.

Sure, he'd told Allie he might be late with the haying, but still... He stuck his head under the shower spigot. She could have swung by where he was working and told him her plans. Was going thirty minutes out of her way too much to ask?

He'd been pacing the length of the front porch for almost an hour when Allie's car finally rounded the corner and drove under the gate. Hannah waved exuberantly from the back seat. Zane took the porch stairs in a single step and strode over to the car. "Where have you been?"

Leaning across the front seat to collect packages, Allie said over her shoulder, "Aspen. Didn't Ruth tell you?" Looking up, she took in his clean clothes. "You finished early."

"Daddy! See my new hat!"

Zane had to smile as his daughter peered from under an oversize floppy blue denim hat. A huge artificial sunflower pinned back the front brim. "I like it." He eyed the packages on the seat beside Hannah's car seat. More sacks rested on the floor. "What's all this?"

"Allie and me went shopping." Hannah raised her feet. "I got sandals," she said proudly.

The brown, clunky shoes were the ugliest Zane had ever seen. He helped Hannah out of the car.

His daughter ran over and put a foot by Allie's feet. "They're like Allie's."

The shoes didn't look any better on Allie's feet. He scowled at the sacks Allie piled in his arms. "Did you buy out the stores?"

"Just about. We had fun, didn't we, Hannah?"

"I got yellow shoes and lots of new clothes for school."

"School?"

"Nursery school," Allie explained. "Once a week to start with."

"Nursery school," Zane echoed blankly.

"I'm gonna play and sing songs, Daddy."

"Nobody said anything to me about nursery school."

En route to the house, Allie blew a kiss at his cheek. "It came up out of the blue. At lunch I ran into a friend who runs a super one. I got Hannah in by promising to work there the mornings Hannah attends. It'll be fun, won't it, Hannah?"

"Allie and me are going to school."

His daughter beamed at his wife who beamed back. Zane reined in his irritation. "You might have consulted me."

"I thought I'd better leap at the opportunity before Darla changed her mind. Nursery school helps socialize kids so they adjust better when they start to kindergarten. I knew you'd want what's best for Hannah."

"Maybe I'd like to be the judge of that," he said tightly.

Opening the door to the house, Allie turned and gave him a puzzled look. "Is something wrong?"

"Nothing's wrong. I just thought, as her father—"

"Look, Daddy!"

"What do—" Impatient with the interruption, Zane turned to Hannah and totally forgot what he'd been asking.

Holding her new hat, Hannah grinned up at him. "I look just like Allie."

Zane couldn't speak. His little baby girl. Her beautiful red hair. Butchered. Her curls. Gone.

His angry roar sent the horses in the near pasture fleeing to the other side.

"It never occurred to me you'd mind," Allie said again. Zane had recovered his temper enough to make it through dinner and Hannah's bedtime, but he clearly continued to seethe.

He scowled at her across the length of the living room. "Where the hell do you get off shearing my daughter's head? She's not some damned sheep. Enrolling her in school was bad enough. I could cancel that. But cutting her hair! What the hell were you thinking, Allie? Tell me. Please. Tell me. What kind of diabolic person shaves a child's head? Never mind. I know what kind. It's your fancy way of getting revenge, isn't it? You can't let the past go, can you?"

"Nobody shaved her head." Staring at him, Allie clutched a pillow to her stomach. How could she have been so wrong?

"You couldn't make me lose my daughter one way, so you decided to steal her. Ply her with new clothes and presents. Turn her into a miniature clone of you." Turning on his heel, Zane stared out the window.

His rigid back sent all kinds of messages. Allie didn't like any of them. She sank back against the sofa. "I wasn't trying—"

"She's my daughter, Allie." He pivoted toward her, his face dark with anger. "Not yours. Mine. I make the decisions about what she wears. I buy her clothes. I decide where and when she goes to school. I decide when and if to cut her hair. Do you understand me? I decide. Hannah's my daughter. She's not your daughter.''

Allie understood too well. Laying the pillow across her lap, she meticulously smoothed out the edges. "I understand. She'll never be my daughter, will she? I misunderstood what you wanted from me. I thought you wanted me to be Hannah's mother. Obviously I was wrong.'' She stood and carefully set the pillow back on the sofa and headed out of the room.

"Where are you going?''

"Upstairs to pack. I can't take everything tonight. Let me know when it's convenient to come by and pick up the rest of my stuff. You can explain to Hannah.''

"Pack?'' Zane followed her up the stairs. "You're leaving?''

In the bedroom, Allie pulled a suitcase from the closet. "Of course, I'm leaving.''

"Why?'' He ran agitated fingers through his hair. "Okay, I'm sorry, I lost my temper. But how could you cut her hair? You had to know I'd hate it.''

She dumped the underwear from the drawer into the suitcase. "If I knew you'd hate it, why would I let her cut it? It wasn't my idea. She wanted it cut.''

"So she could look like you.''

Allie threw some jeans on top of the underwear. "Is that what bothers you? That she wanted to look like me?'' She slammed down the lid to the suitcase. "Are you jealous? Afraid she'll start liking me better than you?"

"Don't be stupid."

"It is stupid, isn't it?" The suitcase wouldn't snap shut. Allie jerked it open and tossed a pair of jeans on the floor. "That's not what this is about. It's about trust. You don't trust me with Hannah. It doesn't matter what I say, you think I'm planning to harm her because of what you did to me. No matter what I do, you'll always be worried about my exacting revenge."

"I didn't say that. All I said was, she's my daughter and I think it's reasonable for you to consult me before making major decisions about her life."

The forbearance in his voice infuriated Allie. Or it would have, if she'd been capable of feeling. His accusations and lack of trust had numbed her hours ago. She prayed the numbness lasted until she escaped this nightmare. Yanking at the wedding ring on her finger, she tossed it on the bed and picked up the suitcase.

Moonie and Amber waited in the hall outside Zane's bedroom. Allie had intended leaving them until tomorrow, but they followed her to the front door. Allie swallowed over the hard, painful lump in her throat. "If you want, I'll try and find another pet for Hannah."

"Forget it. We don't need anything from you."

She would not cry. Not yet. "I know."

In the car, the ranch gate behind her, Allie dialed

the familiar number with shaking fingers. Worth answered. Allie broke out sobbing.

"Allie? Is that you? What's wrong?"

When Worth kept asking if it was her, she realized he couldn't see her nodding her head. "I left," she sobbed.

"Are you in Aspen?"

"On the way." Gulping sobs separated the words.

"Pull over to the side of the road right now and blow your nose. Then quit crying."

"I can't."

"Don't be so damned self-involved," Worth snapped. "Do it. Other people use that road. You can cry all you want when you get to your condo. I'll meet you there. Pull over this second. And stop crying, damn it." He hung up.

Giving a tiny hiccup of tear-laced laughter, Allie pulled over to the side of the road and blew her nose.

Worth must have broken all speed records racing to the condo. The minute Allie drove up, he opened her car door, holding her tight as she collapsed in his arms.

CHAPTER TEN

"He must have married you for a reason," Greeley said in a muffled voice.

"Of course he married me for a reason. He thought having a wife would help if he got entangled in a custody battle. And he wanted sex."

"I think he could get all the sex he wanted without bothering to marry some woman."

"Not the honorable Zane Peters. He has a daughter to think of. Heaven forbid Hannah should ever discover her father fools around. Not to mention the courts in a fight for custody."

Greeley rolled her head out from under Worth's pickup. "Did you ever stop to think maybe you jumped to a few conclusions?"

"I didn't jump. Zane shoved me. You should have heard him, Greeley. The whole time we were married. It was always his house, his horses, his ranch, his daughter, his everything. Not once did he use the word our."

Her sister selected a wrench and disappeared under the pickup again. "Hannah called the ranch house yesterday. Ruth helped her dial the number. She asked Mom where you were."

Allie pressed her lips together. Her one regret was leaving Hannah. Poor little girl. Once again the innocent victim of adults who made a mess of their lives. "I would have had to leave sooner or later. It's better to do it now."

"You could at least call her."

"And tell her what? That I had to leave because her father is afraid I'll strangle her in her bed or something?"

Greeley stuck her head out. "You're in love with him."

"So what?" Allie snapped.

"Did you tell him?"

"Why? So he'd have something else to yell about?"

"You were afraid to tell him. Afraid to trust him."

"I would have gotten around to it," Allie said defensively. "I was waiting for the right time. Trust had nothing to do with it. And what if it did? He let me down before, remember?"

Greeley tapped the wrench on the tire beside her. "Let me see if I have this straight. You're mad at Zane because he doesn't trust you, right?"

"It's not the same thing at all."

"You mean Zane should trust you and one of these days you'll get around to trusting him."

Allie picked up Greeley's oily rag from the shed floor, pulling it between her hands. "If you could have seen his face. Heard the things he said. I'd never do anything to hurt Hannah. Never. How

could he believe I would? I know what he heard me
say at the hospital. I told him I changed my mind.
I agreed to try to make our marriage work. He
doesn't believe any of that. I couldn't stay. We'd
eat away at each other, growing more bitter and
hateful. Leaving was the best thing, the only thing,
I could do. For Hannah. For Zane. For me.''

Zane didn't know why everyone blamed the whole
mess on him. He wasn't the one who slashed off
Hannah's hair. Allie refused to answer her phone or
return his calls. Once he'd reached Cheyenne, but
she'd agreed so coolly and reluctantly to tell Allie
he'd called, he doubted she would. Ruth had been
giving him the silent treatment, while Wally had
taken to short, succinct answers. His mother didn't
believe Hannah's hair could look that bad, and his
father told him he was a damned fool. Zane would
swear, even the damned paint blamed him and was
sulking.

As for Hannah, overnight she'd metamorphosed
from a sweet little girl into a fretful, whining brat.
When she wasn't whining about missing Allie, she
whined about Allie taking Moonie and Amber with
her. Zane had offered to find her a new cat or dog,
but no, his daughter wanted Moonie and Amber.

How did you tell a little girl someone didn't like
her simply because of the circumstances of her
birth?

He'd tried to forget Allie admitting she resented
and disliked Hannah. Wanted to forget because he

wanted to sleep with Allie. His father was right. He was a damned fool, just not in the way his father meant.

Zane couldn't deny that Allie had been honest about one thing at least. She'd flat out admitted she wanted revenge.

How the hell could she turn around and blame him for wanting to protect his daughter from her?

Across the table, Hannah kicked the legs of her booster chair. "I don't like this." She shoved her plate away. "I don't wanna eat it."

Zane counted silently to ten before answering patiently. "You like macaroni and cheese." He'd asked Ruth to fix it, knowing it was one of Hannah's favorite foods.

"I hate it. Allie wouldn't make me eat stuff I hate."

"Allie's not here anymore."

"I want Allie back."

Zane had no answer for that. The truth was, so did he.

If only Allie would try to understand. Hannah was his daughter. He'd fed her and changed her diapers and rocked her to sleep and bathed her. He'd coaxed medicine down her tiny throat and sat up all night with her when she had earaches. When she'd had a temperature of 104 degrees, he'd wiped her with cool cloths and prayed for her recovery. This small, exquisite person had come into the world because of him, and she depended on him to keep her safe and well.

Hannah leaned back and plopped her feet on the table.

"What do you think you're doing, young lady? And don't tell me Allie let you put your feet on the dinner table."

Hannah pushed out her lower lip. "They're ugly toes."

Zane stood and walked around the table. Gently moving Hannah's feet, he said, "They're not ugly toes, but they don't belong on the table."

"They're ugly." She kicked the table leg and didn't look at him. "I want Allie to fix them."

Zane caught one of her feet. The toenail polish had mostly worn off. "I have an idea. Why don't I paint your toenails?"

Hannah jerked her foot away. "Allie took the polish."

"We can buy more."

"Don't want more," Hannah said mulishly. "Want Allie's."

Zane went back to his chair. "Allie's not coming back," he said quietly. Hannah started crying, the sobs ripping apart his heart. He forced himself to eat.

He'd give Hannah anything he could.

He couldn't give her Allie.

The macaroni stuck in his throat and he thought he'd choke trying to swallow it. Doggedly he kept eating. Across the table Hannah's crying continued unabated.

If only Allie had been patient. He loved her. He

would have come to trust her eventually. If she'd loved him, she would have been patient. She would have understood. It wasn't as if he was testing her. He'd needed a little time.

He'd thought they were going to make it this time. Allie was right. There was no happily ever after for them.

He'd never eat macaroni and cheese again.

Zane knew the approaching pickup couldn't be Allie. That didn't stop him from hoping.

Greeley halted the pickup a few feet from the barn. "Hi."

He gripped the pitchfork tightly. "She forget something?"

Greeley raised an eyebrow. "What happened to pleasantries like hello, how are you?"

Zane locked his jaw in place. He didn't give a damn about pleasantries.

She uttered a short laugh. "Thanks for asking, Zane, I'm fine. How are you?"

"What do you want?"

"Cheyenne sent me. She wanted to come, but Thomas has absolutely forbidden her to interfere. Ordinarily that wouldn't stop her, but she's a newlywed and letting Thomas think he's running the show."

The undoubted truth of Greeley's words forced reluctant laughter from Zane. "Poor sucker."

"You ought to know how it is. The Lassiter

women can be real pains in the neck. Mom and I excepted, of course.''

''I suppose you'll tell me in your own sweet time what you want.''

''I understand you have a birthday coming up in a couple of weeks. I brought you an early present.''

''From Allie?'' He couldn't suppress a tiny burst of hope.

Greeley gave him a mocking look. ''At this point, if I were you, if I received anything from Allie, I'd put it in a bucket of water and call the bomb squad.''

He tried to keep the disappointment from his face.

''I swear, Zane,'' Greeley said in disgust, ''you are the world's biggest idiot. If you love her that much, why'd you run her off?''

''Who said I love her?''

Greeley shook her head and handed him a large envelope. ''Cheyenne found these in Allie's trash can. Allie had planned to give them to you for your birthday. Cheyenne said if you breathe one word of this to Thomas, she'll skin you alive.'' Putting the pickup in gear, Greeley reversed and was gone before Zane could ask what was in the envelope.

Divorce papers would come from an attorney.

Leaning the pitchfork against the barn wall, he slowly pulled off his gloves, dropping them on the ground. He turned the envelope over. Trying to place the name on the front side, it took a second before the word "Photographer" penetrated his brain.

He ripped open the envelope. Photographer's proofs rained to the ground. Zane bent down and retrieved them one by one.

The first few proofs portrayed Hannah. She sat on a lush carpet of grass reading a book, one bare foot propped on the knee of her other leg. Zane had seen her sit that way so often, he visualized her toes wiggling as she read the book, making up the story as she turned the pages. Sprawling behind her, Moonie, acting as her back rest, gave every indication of listening intently.

Zane moved on to the second set of poses. If the first pictures made him smile, these made him want to laugh. Or cry. The photographer had snapped Allie and Hannah blowing soap bubbles. Allie, on her knees in the grass, concentrated on blowing a bubble that had already reached monstrous size. Hannah, her own bubble wand forgotten, watched the bubble grow, her eyes as big as the bubble. The hat Allie wore matched Hannah's floppy blue denim hat.

In the third pose Allie and Hannah had collapsed in a heap on the grass while dozens of effervescent bubbles rained down on them. Zane could almost hear Hannah giggling helplessly. He could only imagine how the photographer managed to take several shots of the scene before the bubbles popped or floated away. Allie must have worn herself out blowing bubbles.

There was only one version of the final pose. Hannah sat sleepily on Allie's lap. Hannah's hat lay on the ground. Her hair had already been cut.

With her hair short, Hannah looked a lot like Allie. He hadn't noticed before. The significance of Hannah wanting short hair belatedly occurred to him. The children Hannah knew all had mothers. His sister's children. His friends' children. Davy. Hannah was bright. She must have heard over and over again someone say a child looked like his or her mother. Having a mother who played with angels couldn't compete with having a mother to look like. The photographic proof blurred.

He'd been so mixed up loving Allie and being afraid to trust her, he hadn't realized Hannah had picked herself a new mother. The last proof clearly pointed out what else he'd blindly missed. The love on Allie's face as she looked down at Hannah. Allie couldn't have known the photographer was taking the last picture. She'd never have allowed such naked feeling to be photographed.

He was a damned fool.

Allie could love the most miserable, ill-begotten, mangy, snarling beast. What the hell had made him think she couldn't love Hannah?

"Whatcha got, Daddy?" Hannah came running up and pulled down his arm to see what he held. "How come you got the pictures? Is today your birthday?"

"No." Suddenly he grinned. "Yes, in a way, it

is, honey. If a birthday is the first day of a person's
life, then today's my birthday.''

"We gonna have cake and ice cream?''

Swooping her up with one arm, Zane squeezed
her. ''Not today. We'll have cake and ice cream on
my other birthday.''

"I want it now.''

"Now we have things to do. We have to pack.
I've decided I'm going to Texas, and you're going
to stay with Allie.''

"I am?'' At his nod, Hannah threw her arms
around his neck. ''I love you, Daddy.'' She leaned
back and looked in his face. ''Did you see it? Allie
said you would.''

"See what?''

"The love in the pictures.''

"I saw it.''

That evening, as he packed, Hannah thumbed
through the photographer's proofs. ''I can't see the
love, Daddy.''

Zane pointed to Allie's face. ''There. See how
much she loves you.''

"That's my love,'' Hannah said scornfully. ''I
can't see yours. You know. 'Cuz Allie and I love
you.''

Zane's heart skipped a beat. ''What makes you
think Allie loves me? Did she say she loves me?''

"Daddy,'' Hannah said in a very adult tone of
voice, ''of course Allie loves you. Davy said so.''

Allie couldn't imagine who would be ringing her
condo doorbell at six-thirty in the morning.

Dragging herself out of bed, she shrugged into her bathrobe. Moonie stood in front of the door trying to wag off his tail. Amber had pushed aside the front curtains and meowed loudly. Allie stretched. It must be Worth. Yawning, she opened the door.

"Good morning, Allie. Hope I didn't get you out of bed."

"Hi, Allie."

She stared at the father and daughter standing on her doorstep. Two faces grinned back. Allie blinked her eyes. She must be dreaming.

Zane pushed her to one side and set a small suitcase on the floor. Going down on one knee, he gave Hannah a swift hug. "Okay, have fun." Standing, he drew Allie into his arms and hugged her briefly. "You, too. See you in several days or so."

"What is going on? Zane?" she yelled after him as he headed for the door.

"The paperwork's in her suitcase." He edged away as he talked. "Permission slips, power of attorney, should be everything you need. We'll switch the ranch title over to both our names when I return. We can talk about adoption then."

Allie grabbed his arm. "Don't you dare walk out of here. Where are you going? What are you talking about?"

"I have to run, honey. I'm delivering some horses down in Texas. My cell phone number is with the rest of the stuff if you need it. Wally's going with me. The hands know what to do, but if anything comes up, you're in charge out at the ranch.'' He shook off her arm.

"Bye, Daddy.'' Hannah raised her face. "Kiss!''

Zane obliged her with a loud smacking kiss. Then he smiled at Allie. She didn't mean to kiss him, but somehow she was in his arms, her mouth pressed to his. He stepped back. "Gotta go. I'll miss my two best girls, but I'll be back as soon as I can.'' He turned steady eyes on Allie. "You can count on that.''

Allie felt like a tornado had blown through her condo. "You're going off and leaving Hannah? With me?''

"Sure. Ruth's going to Texas with us. Her cousin lives down there.'' He turned to Hannah. "Don't forget what I told you.'' And then he was running down the sidewalk.

By the time Allie had gathered her scattered wits, the pickup and large horse trailer had disappeared around the corner at the end of the block. Allie slowly shut her door and gazed down at Hannah. "Well,'' she said, totally disoriented.

Hannah beamed at her.

"Have you had breakfast?''

Hannah nodded vigorously.

"I suppose your father told you to be good.''

The little girl shook her head and giggled.

"What did he tell you?''

"He said you're my new mama. I got to call you Mama.'' Her joyful grin lit up the entire room.

Allie pressed a hand over her mouth. The action did nothing to stop her flowing tears.

He had sweaty palms. A person would think he was a damned teenager. Allie had kissed him goodbye. He clung to that fact. Nothing else gave him hope. She hadn't contacted him. He'd made all the phone calls, calling often enough to talk to her and Hannah. Not so often as to make Allie think he was checking up on her.

The telephone calls told him nothing. They'd discussed the weather. Hannah had blue toenails and her own bubble bath. Raspberry bubblegum scent or something. Zane thought little girls should smell like little girls, but Hannah was thrilled.

Every time he phoned, he intended to tell Allie he loved her before he hung up. Each time he lost his nerve. Allie hadn't exactly gushed with love, either.

Leaving Ruth and Wally in Texas, he'd made good time back. Two days ago he'd called Allie and said he'd be home early tomorrow, but the closer Zane got to Colorado, the harder his foot pressed on the gas pedal. Driving late last night, he'd been on the road this morning long before the sun rose.

Zane didn't know if Hannah had told Allie he'd told his daughter Allie was her new mother. He'd been afraid to ask. Neither Hannah nor Allie brought it up.

His phone calls usually found Allie and Hannah at the ranch. As he drove through the gate, Zane hadn't made up his mind about the significance of Allie staying at the ranch. Maybe she thought Hannah would be happier in her own bed. Maybe it meant nothing more than Allie taking seriously her responsibilities as far as running the ranch in his absence. Caring for Hannah and running the ranch could be duties she felt had been forced upon her, but she was carrying them out for lack of anyone else to act as caretaker.

The phone calls disturbed him. Hannah had giggled a lot, but said little about what they were doing. Allie had been, not exactly distant, but noncommittal.

Allie's car sat in front of the house. Zane parked the truck and trailer by the barn. He'd unhitch later. Taking the porch steps in a single bound, he opened the front door.

"Daddy, no!" Hannah stopped three-quarters of the way down the staircase and gave him a look of utter dismay. "Go 'way!"

It wasn't the reception he expected.

Hannah spun around and charged up the stairs. "Allie-mama! Allie-mama! Daddy's home! He can't come home now!"

Moonie looked at Zane then trotted up the stairs in Hannah's wake.

Music blared from upstairs. Allie's voice came over the din. "I can't hear you, honey. What did you say?"

"Daddy's home!"

"Turn down the music. Now, what did you say?"

"She said her father's home."

The jeans-clad bottom he'd been admiring whipped around. The look of dismay on Allie's face mimicked Hannah's. "What are you doing here? You aren't supposed to be home until tomorrow."

"You ruined it, Daddy. You ruined our surprise."

Two outraged faces glared at him. He'd thought at least Hannah would be glad to see him. Unable to face their scowling faces, he looked around the room, which had been his parents' bedroom, then Kim's.

Every piece of furniture had been removed. An old-fashioned floral wallpaper replaced the psychedelic wallpaper. Polished wooden floors gleamed in the sunlight coming through the uncurtained windows. Zane looked up.

Mirrored tiles reflected his surprised face. And reflected the two females in his life. Showing him what he'd missed in his disappointment at their reception of his early arrival. Both wore ragged, paint-stained clothes. More white paint covered Hannah's arms than the baseboards he'd obviously interrupted Allie painting. Judging by the varicolored paint splotches in Allie's hair, she'd painted more than baseboards. A wide streak of white paint ran down her face.

Bubbles of laughter and love rose in him like heady champagne. "I love you two," he said.

Hannah smiled at him in the mirror. "I love you, Daddy." Her smile vanished as she stuck her little fists on nonexistent hips. "How come you spoiled our surprise? We was gonna get beautiful for you. Allie-mama said."

"You are beautiful." His gaze went to Allie's in the mirror. "Both of you. I love you so much."

Allie grimaced. "It must be love if you think I look beautiful." She tugged at her messy, paint-splattered hair. "I look like something out of a horror movie."

"You look beautiful. You look like my wife. You look like my daughter's mother." He laughed, because if he didn't, he'd cry. "Her Allie-mama."

Allie rapidly blinked her eyes in a losing effort to hold back the tears he saw glittering in her eyes. "You look like a man who's been long days on the road and could use a meal, a shower, and a hug and kiss from his wife and daughter," she said. "Not necessarily in that order."

"There you are." Allie walked into the bedroom saying, "I think I'm going to have to cut the paint out of my hair." She stopped short. "What is this?"

"Hannah's old mattress." Zane threw two pillows on the mattress. "Since she's taken over my room, we have to sleep somewhere."

He didn't sound critical, but Allie rushed to explain. "Hannah needed a bigger room. I've been sleeping in her old bed. We don't have to sleep in here on the floor."

"The way you piled all the furniture from in here into that room, I could barely breathe in there."

"That's your fault for coming home too early." He looked so sexy with bare feet and no shirt, she hardly knew what she was saying. "Worth and Thomas are coming tomorrow to bring down your parents' furniture from the attic. The Taylors want the rug and stuff that was in here. I told them you'd trailer it over."

"They want it, they can come get it," Zane said flatly.

Allie didn't bother to point out the obvious. Regardless of her and Zane's opinions of the Taylors and their past willingness to use Hannah for their own financial gain, they were, and always would be, Hannah's grandparents. Allie had used Kim's bedroom furnishings as an olive branch, one which the Taylors had chosen to accept. The fact that neither Sean Doyle nor custody of Hannah had been mentioned made Allie hopeful the Taylors had pragmatically accepted Zane would be keeping Hannah, and if they wanted any relationship with her, they'd have to deal with Zane. Allie was realistic enough to assume the Taylors hoped, by being friendly, they might wheedle a dollar here and there out of Zane. Accordingly, she said, "We'll see."

Zane made a derisive sound. "Meaning you're a newlywed and letting me think I'm running the show."

"What's that supposed to mean?" she asked indignantly.

"Ask Greeley." He walked around the mattress and rested his hands on her shoulders, gazing steadily down into her face. "Allie, coming home from Texas, I was scared silly I'd messed up so badly you'd never let me in your life again. I need you, not for Hannah's sake, for mine. Living these past five years without you was like going through life with part of me missing. I can't do that again. I promise you, honey, I'll never let you down again. I love you, Alberta Peters, more than I'll ever be able to tell you."

"I love you." Allie wrapped her arms around his bare middle, warmth and contentment stealing over her. "We came so close to losing our love. This time we know how special love is, and we'll work harder to keep ours alive and growing."

Zane rested his forehead on her head. "One other thing... After Kim and I married, well, I couldn't make myself sleep with her in this room. I'd expected to share it with you. Kim and I...well, we used the guest room." He paused. "After a few weeks, I moved back to my room and she moved in here. She... We, uh, lived separate lives after that."

Zane's faltering explanation peeled back the last blinders Allie wore about Zane's first marriage. In her mind she saw Kim and Zane living in the same house, strangers, bound together only by their child and their suffering. For the first time Allie truly comprehended what kind of hellish existence he and Kim had endured. Compassion for Kim erased the last of her anger. "That's past," Allie said firmly.

"Kim gave you a wondrous gift, your daughter. We can both be thankful for that."

"I don't deserve you," Zane said in a thick voice.

Allie tightened her grasp. "Too bad. You're stuck with me. Now, are you going to talk all night, or are we going to bed?" She felt Zane's startled movement, then he slid his hands over her shoulders, his fingers performing an erotic dance, which sent desire shimmering over her skin.

"Anxious to try out that mirrored ceiling, are you?" he teased in a low, seductive voice.

Embarrassment heated her face. "It's going to take a jackhammer to get those things off. It would have made more sense to wait until a new ceiling had been installed before I wallpapered and painted."

"I didn't marry you for your good sense," Zane murmured provocatively against her neck, slipping off her robe.

"I know." Allie closed her eyes, savoring the delicious sensations Zane aroused. "You wanted to sleep with me."

"No." He slid his thumbs under the straps of her new nightgown. "I needed someone to paint Hannah's toenails."

"Liar." Allie ran her palms up his arms. "You wanted me back because the sex is very good."

"Does that mean I've changed good into very good?"

"You haven't changed anything." Allie curved

her arms around his neck. "It's always been very good." She smiled up at him and a glint overhead caught her eye. "Turn off the light and let's go to bed."

"If we turn out the light, we can't see the mirrors."

Allie kissed his collarbone. "Exactly."

"Losing your nerve?" He laughed softly at her nod. "Wear this and you'll be adequately dressed." He reached into his pocket, then held out his hand.

The wedding ring gleamed in the light. Allie slipped it on her fourth finger. "This is all I need, isn't it?" Using her body, she pressed him backward.

They tumbled on the mattress together, laughing and loving.

"Allie."

The insistent calling of her name wakened Allie. She rolled over. Zane wasn't in bed. "Zane?"

"Over here." He stood at the uncurtained window. "I want to show you something."

Finding her robe on the floor, Allie shrugged into it and joined him at the window. "What are you doing?"

"I got up to get a blanket. You never let me finish making up the bed." He pulled her close to his side, his arm wrapped snugly around her. "Watch."

She loved the feel of his hand on her hip. Closing her eyes, she inhaled the scent of his soap.

His lips touched her hair. "You're supposed to be watching."

Turning toward him, she rose on her toes and pressed a kiss into the dent in the middle of his chin. "There's nothing to see," she murmured against his skin.

"Behave yourself and do as you're told." Zane firmly turned her toward the open window and pulled her back against his hard body. "I'm trying to show you something."

She didn't see a thing. "The ranch light's burned out."

"That's how I happened to see it."

Mounds of dark clouds scudded across the sky, uncovering, now covering an occasional star. Allie picked out the distant silhouette of the Elk Mountains. A small breeze brought the smell of rain and jangled the leaves on the large cottonwood tree. The air hinted at coming winter. Zane must have felt her tiny shiver because he enfolded her in his warm arms. His loving arms.

"Here it comes," he said quietly.

Overhead a large golden orb slid from behind a wall of clouds and bathed the ranch yard in light. The moon's bright glow spotlighted Greeley's sculpture, throwing immense shadows of the three metal horses on the ground. Shadows from the swaying cottonwood limbs superimposed themselves on the horse shadows, giving movement and life to the larger shadows. Three phantom horses pranced in the yard.

"Hannah's family," Allie said in delight. "You and me and Hannah."

Zane's arms tightened. "Look. There to the right."

A small bush threw a perfect silhouette of a miniature horse. No, not a miniature horse. A baby horse, a foal. The shadow blended with the other images.

"A family of four," Zane said.

Allie could only nod.

They watched the four shadows cavort in the moonlight until the moon went back into hiding, and the shadows merged with the night.

"Well." Zane cleared his throat. "What do you think, Mrs. Peters?"

"I think we'd better start thinking about giving Greeley a new reason to fire up her welding tools."

Zane could have told Allie he'd been thinking about her having his baby from the instant he'd seen her at Cheyenne's wedding. He kept his mouth shut. He'd been a fool, but he wasn't that big a fool. What was it Greeley said? Something about newlyweds letting their spouses think they're running the show. He ran his hands over Allie's breasts and down her stomach until he heard her catch her breath. "Whatever you say, honey."

Allie laughed, not the least bit taken in by his docile remark. Zane laughed with her. They both knew they were partners. In love and in life.

EPILOGUE

THE low call of a homeward-bound owl wakened Allie from a light sleep. Outside, false dawn touched the sky with gray. Zane shifted his body so his bottom touched her hip, then his breathing returned to the slow rhythm of deep slumber. Basking in his warmth, Allie contentedly placed her hands on her abdomen. If the mirrored tiles hadn't been removed from the ceiling, they'd undoubtedly reflect a silly smile on her face.

Married the better part of nine months, she could write a testimonial to the virtues of matrimony. Hannah was the light of her father's eyes and a joy to Allie. Several women had been hired to help at the tour agency giving her and Cheyenne more time to spend with their families.

Family. Allie put that thought aside to savor later.

First she had to finish listing the virtues of matrimony. The ranch was green and fecund with precious new colts frisking around the pastures. Amber tolerated Hannah's new white kitten, while Mooney adored the tiny creature, named Ice Cream by Hannah.

Allie turned her head and surveyed the dark head

on the next pillow. The best part of her marriage. She wanted to slide her hands over Zane's warm back and whisper words of love into his ear until he wakened to love her. She resisted the urge, gifting him with another hour of sleep. Their loving echoed everything good about their union.

She slid carefully out of bed before temptation overcame her good intentions. Wrapping her robe around her, she padded on bare feet to the open window and breathed in the cool June air. A few stars dawdled overhead and high above the Elk Mountains.

The ranch light in the yard illuminated Greeley's sculpture. Allie smiled and lightly touched her stomach.

Zane knew the second she left the bed. He flipped back the blanket and joined her at the window, covering her hand where it rested on her abdomen. "How's little Harmony?"

"I didn't mean to waken you." Allie leaned against him, her body warm and soft. "Harmony could be a boy."

"Nope." He chuckled softly. "I like the idea of a whole troop of females running around taking care of me."

"Chauvinist." After a second she asked, "Do you care whether the baby's a boy or a girl?"

"I want a healthy baby and a healthy mom," he said firmly, wrapping his arms around her. "When are you going to announce the news?"

"I want to let Cheyenne have the spotlight for a while longer."

"That's not the real reason you're keeping it a secret. She'll be thrilled you're pregnant, too." He wanted to shout the news from the top of Aspen Mountain.

"You know me too well. All right. I like it being our private secret for now."

"Better not let it go too long." He rested his chin on her head. "Greeley'll get so busy she won't have time to add to our sculpture." He felt her body tense. "You're worried about her."

"Don't be silly. She's perfectly capable of handling her own affairs."

"Un-huh. That's why we and the Steeles had to rush to Aspen this evening to dine at St. Chris's and, not so incidentally, inspect this Quint Damian fellow."

"You don't know how it is with Greeley."

"You told me we were going to dinner to keep Cheyenne from interfering."

"Sometimes Cheyenne is right, you know."

"And this is one of those times," Zane said in resignation.

"Did you see what Greeley wore to meet him?"

"I'm married, not dead," he teased. "I never realized what a hot little number she is."

"Poor Zane. Married to someone who wants to sleep half the day, has a craving for root beer floats and will no doubt grow to be the size of St. Chris's."

"I'll love every minute of it." He caressed her stomach. "Having my baby growing inside you is the sexiest thing I can think of." It suddenly occurred to him his teasing might have upset her. "I certainly don't find you any less desirable because you're pregnant. I was joking about Greeley being hot."

"She only dresses like that when she's trying to prove how independent and tough she is. That nothing scares her. Worth calls it her whistling-in-the-dark disguise." Allie sighed. "I never really appreciated what Mom went through raising four of us. Now, with Hannah and the baby... I want them to be safe and happy, but I know I won't be able to protect them always from hurt." She hesitated. "I think Mom's worried about Greeley."

His knowledge of the Lassiter women warned him what was coming next. "You're going to mess in Greeley's business."

"Do you mind?"

He thought about Greeley bringing him the pictures. "No. Do what you have to do. If you need my help, I'm here."

"I know."

The trust in her voice almost unmanned him. He loved this woman so much. The sun still lay below the eastern horizon. They had time. He nibbled her nape. "Can we go back to bed? In case you haven't noticed, I'm stark naked and shaking with the cold."

Allie laughed quietly. "Is that what's going on?"

He loved her laugh. "I'll be glad to show you exactly what's going on, Mrs. Peters." Scooping her carefully into his arms, he carried her to the bed and gently laid her down.

"You don't think you can talk about how hot my sister is one minute and make love to me the next, do you?" she asked in mock indignation.

He lay down beside her. "I didn't know how much love and laughter and tenderness and goodness and joy could be in a man's life until you married me."

The love in her eyes ruined the scowl she tried to put on her face. "Do you really think all those pretty words will soften you up so you can have your way with me?"

"No." He slipped his hand inside her robe. "I think this will persuade you to let me have my way with you."

She needed very little persuasion.

Later, watching Allie's face as their daughter skipped into their bedroom, trailed by a dog and two cats, Zane did what he did every morning. He fell in love with his wife all over again.

Look for Greeley's story. Coming soon in Harlequin Romance.

HARLEQUIN PRESENTS®

HARLEQUIN PRESENTS
men you won't be able to resist
falling in love with...

HARLEQUIN PRESENTS
women who have feelings
just like your own...

HARLEQUIN PRESENTS
powerful passion in
exotic international settings...

HARLEQUIN PRESENTS
intense, dramatic stories that will keep you
turning to the very last page...

HARLEQUIN PRESENTS
The world's bestselling romance series!

Harlequin® Historical

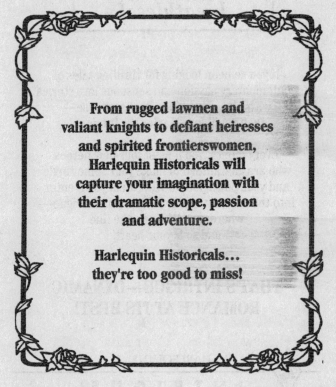

From rugged lawmen and
valiant knights to defiant heiresses
and spirited frontierswomen,
Harlequin Historicals will
capture your imagination with
their dramatic scope, passion
and adventure.

Harlequin Historicals...
they're too good to miss!

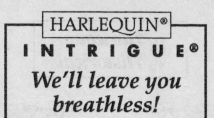